65½

WHITE TEETH

OKOT p'BITEK

HEINEMANN KENYA

Published by
Heinemann Kenya Ltd.
Brick Court
Mpaka Road/Woodvale Grove
P.O. Box 45314,
Nairobi.

First published in 1953 as *Lak Tar*

ISBN 9966-46-445-X

Printed by
General Printers Ltd., Homa Bay Road,
P.O. Box 18001, Nairobi, Kenya.

ACKNOWLEDGEMENTS

"The longest journey begins with the first step," goes a wise English saying. Everything in this world has a beginning and an end, so was with my late husband Professor Dr. Okot p'Bitek, when he plunged into the literary world.

The book *White Teeth* you are embarking on was the very first novel the late Professor wrote in his youthful years to make a breakthrough into the world of writing, when it was first published in his mother tongue, Acoli, in 1953. It was written at the time of my husband's most glamorous era when he was full of courage, ambition and hope for a better and promising future. Most important, it was at the time before Uganda became independent and publications of vernacular literatures were limited to religious materials, or exceptionally good manuscripts which were hard to come by.

The publication of *Lak Tar* in vernacular came at a transitional period when traditional culture was in great conflict with modern culture. The book mainly dwells on the upheavals of bridewealth which were racking the social and economic setting of the Acoli community, due to the introduction of a monetary economy brought about by modern civilisation. An Acholi chief, *Rwot* Olwa of Attiak, made a historic mark in his attempts to limit the ever increasing demands for bridewealth, when he made a decree throughout Acoliland, limiting brideprice to two cows and two goats. Several by-laws enacted by local chiefs and Acoli District Council thereafter were vain efforts to curb the economic demands through bridewealth, which perish among the Acoli to date.

This phenomenon drove many young men from their Acoli homeland to look for employment in various corners of Uganda, especially in Kampala, where the youths were faced with a lot of adventures, full of suffering in majority cases. Most of these young men returned home bare handed. The few lucky ones may return with some thing that could afford them wives.

Okeca Ladwong who is a chief character in this book, shows the lifestyle of a cross section of the suffering youths who were driven out of Acoliland by poverty to remote corners of Uganda with the hope that they would strike some luck in the course of their adventure and one day return home with something tangible that would improve their social and economic status, only to run into seas of problems ahead.

It is my greatest pleasure to introduce the translated version of my late husband's novel, *Lak Tar*. The book was his first step in the long journey he travelled into the literary world. Okot worked on the translation of this book himself, early 1982, before he died and was pleased to have completed the translation, although he often complained the translation had lost the flavour the book had in Acoli. He then submitted two chapters of his translation to be published in the *Artist the Ruler* (Heinemann, 1986) as he went on to polish the translation to his satisfaction. He died before he put the finishing touches on the *White Teeth* version. I am grateful to Lubwa P'chong who helped with the last bit.

We were all saddened when Okot suddenly left us in July 1982. But we are proud as members of the Bitek family that he still lives on, in the world of literature.

I wish to pay special tribute on behalf of the Bitek family to all those friends who have grown and lived with my late husband Okot p'Bitek and shared thoughts in various capacities. I am also indebted on behalf of the family, to those who might have crossed swords with my late husband in the "literary arena" during his hectic and dynamic time in the world of arts purely in genuine debate.

I would also like to express my personal thanks and gratitude and that of the Bitek family to the following persons who have remained persistent friends to the family during my husband's life-time and after his sad and sudden demise:

Gerald Moore; Aida Southall; David Rubadiri; David Cook; Lubwa P'chong; John Ruganda; Phillip and Paula Foster; Wole Soyinka; Gacheche Waruingi; J.P. Clark; Oyin Ogumba; Chinua Achebe; Professor and Mrs. Ogot; Atieno Odhiambo; Dr. and Mrs. Dalizu; Samson Lubwa Too; Mr. and Mrs. Lakana Omal (Adoktoo), the Reverend Father Dr. Anthony Okello; Taban lo Liyong; Sister Olga; Sister Lucilla; Okello Oculi; Mr. and Mrs. Oceng and Wod Okello Lawoko.

Caroline Auma Okot p'Bitek,
Gulu,
UGANDA, (1988)

FOREWORD

The original version of this book, written in Acoli language, of *Lak Tar Miyo Kinyero Wilobo* (White Teeth make us laugh on earth), often shortened to *Lak Tar* (White Teeth), was first published in 1953 by the defunct East African Literature Bureau, Eagle Press.

At the time of its publication, the late Professor Okot p'Bitek was only twenty-two years old and it was perhaps one of the earliest published novels in East Africa.

The novel was a commentary on the changes which were taking place in the custom of bridewealth. Bridewealth was a major social concern right across the board in the Acoli Community, and with the arrival of the monetary economy, people started charging exorbitant prices, sometimes in thousands of shillings. This was quite a sum in that kind of poverty-stricken part of the country. Later the Acoli District Council got concerned and passed numerous by-laws, one of them fixing bridewealth to five hundred shillings, in those transitional years, but in vain. A story was told of a member of the then Acoli District Council. When a prospective son-in-law came to marry his daughter, he demanded thousands of shillings for the daughter. When his attention was drawn to the by-law which he supported, his cool comment was: "In that case, you can go and marry the daughter of law."

So the novel was mainly a condemnation of such practices and this condemnation is still valid in 1980s. I know of a man who paid a quarter of a million Uganda shillings plus thirty head of cattle because the woman was a university graduate in 1982.

But the book was also a condemnation of corruption in Kampala; of the breakdown of the clan system, and of the exploitation of Africans by Asians in those material days. And the betrayal of Okeca Ladwong, an Acoli by Ogwang, a Langi by tribe, was a subtle commentary on the age old conflict between the Acoli and Langi tribes of Northern Uganda.

The translation of the novel from Acoli to English by the author later in the wake of 1980s shortly before he died had not been an easy work and Okot p'Bitek grumbled insidiously as he laboured with the translation complaining that due to lack of suitable terms and vocabularies that befitted the colloquial Acoli terms, the English version was likely to lose a lot of meaning at the end.

I have had the honour of sharing a lot of thoughts with the late professor during the busy days of this translated work. Two chapters of this novel, *White Teeth,* were published in the *Artist the Ruler,* published in 1986. During my study tours which took me to the University of Durham, U.K. and the University of Iowa, U.S.A., in 1987, I had the pleasure and opportunity of reading chapters of the translated work of the *White Teeth* to associates of different cultural backgrounds, the contents of which generated a lot of interest and discussions on the book content.

Okot p'Bitek wrote a number of books which were read world-wide by people of different culture and academic excellence. *White Teeth* will unfold a deeper understanding of the author revealing his critical outlook to Acoli culture he had had right from his youthful days when he made a debut into a literary world. The book will also reveal to the reader that Okot p'Bitek was not only a defender of cultural values but was vehement to any cultural revolution, inherited or acquired, which is repugnant to social justice.

I have no doubt *White Teeth* will generate a lot of interest with comments and debates.

LUBWA P'chong
INSTITUTE OF TEACHER EDUCATION
P.O. BOX 1
KYAMBOGO, KAMPALA
UGANDA.

WHITE TEETH

A Novel by
OKOT p'BITEK
Translated from his first Acoli book,
LAK TAR.

In everlasting memories of
    the late Father,
Zebedayo Opil Bitek and;
    the late Mother,
Serina Lacaa Bitek:

Whose careful hands and wisdom
groomed the late Professor Dr.
Okot p'Bitek and armed him with
cultural love and traditional
knowledge, zeal and affection
for his heritage in the deep
and wide seas of the ever
changing world. . . .

CHAPTER ONE

My name is Okeca Ladwong, but friends call me Atuk. Atuk is my *mwoc**:
   Atuk, *Otuk ruk*!*
   You disturbed *ten**
   In your mother-in-law's hut.
   Your eye-lids are heavy
   On account of food
   Your eye-lids are dark
   Because you do not want to share
   The carcass of the cow
   That had died of dysentery.
It is I, Atuk, speaking. I come from Patiko:
   We are lions
   We are an okra dish
   A little dish of okra
   Finishes a big lump of *kwon**
   We are softeners
   We cool you off
   However fierce you may be
   We are lions
   We of Patiko are hot
   Hot like red pepper
   We are itchy!
My father's name was Ojok Lapok. His *mwoc,* White Teeth. He shouted:
   It is white teeth
   That make us laugh in this world!
Short and thick-necked, my father, they called him, *Oyeng-yeng,* Earthshaker, for when he walked, the ground shook.

My mother comes from Atyak, fondly referred to as Lwani. Tall, big-chested. She was taller than her husband, and they call her, Abalo Muca. She never cooks much. Her nickname is *Tyena-teda,* my feet are my cooks, for she eats where her feet carry her to.

Odora Obal-lim is my father's elder brother:

Your tobacco bag is empty
You provoke a mamba
In the hole of *mwok* ant-eater
A black billy-goat has broken the water pot!

He was a bit taller than his brother, but gaunt, and there was never a man meaner than him. His name, Obal-lim, aptly means, "Waster of wealth". He never parts willingly with anything he owns!

White teeth, that was my father's *mwoc.* When I was a child, I did not understand what it meant, for I thought people laughed because they were happy, or because a funny story had softened their insides. But when I grew up, I realised it was the white of teeth that forced men to laugh!

The suffering I endured at the hands of my father's brother because of the daughter of Gurucenycio Obiya Balmoi Cotta, and the suffering I went through in a distant land, should have blocked my throat completely and stopped me from laughing any more in this world. But the whiteness of my teeth, not happiness, not pleasures, not the softness of my inside; my white teeth force me to laugh, for fear that girls might think my teeth are rotten and rusty like those of the bull edible rat.

It is my white teeth that make me laugh still. But when people see and hear me laugh, they say: "Ah, the son of Ojok is a very cheerful and happy man!" Others say: "The son of Ojok is a funny man indeed!" My age-mates laugh at me when I laugh and say I must be very odd because I laugh when I am suffering so much! And the girls say: "But Atuk is not an ordinary boy; he is so special!" I am not cheerful, not odd, not funny, nor am I special. It is the white of my teeth that makes me laugh.

One morning many years ago, the women in our homestead

set out for the wilderness to collect sheanuts to make shea-butter. They started from home when the teeth of the morning sun were getting sharp, because you do not go to collect shea-nuts on the hills too early in the morning for fear of fiends and wild animals that roam the hills at night and early morning. This was towards the end of the wet season, and the *acil* grass was heavily laden with seeds. My mother's womb was very ripe too, with me.

They collected a lot of sheanuts, until each woman had a big basketful. They then gathered under a *kibuu* tree to rest, and to eat the sweet, fleshy fruits. Just as they were ready to start for home, heavy storm burst upon them from beyond the Ajulu Hill. The winds were furious like fighting elephants, trumpeting, tearing, pushing, pulling.... The women rushed into a cave; a hyena's den.

The rains refused to stop. The women lamented; some for foodstuffs they had put out to dry; some for their hungry children at home; some for their husbands who went out early in the morning to dig on empty stomachs; others wondering what dish they would prepare on their return home. But Oba-lim's youngest wife was perfectly happy. Abalo was happy because her hut leaked. She had cut the grass for the repair, but her husband refused to re-thatch it because, he said, the woman had refused to give him beer she had brewed. Abalo had made the beer to sell and use the money to pay her son's poll tax. Her son had already been locked up in a cell to await payment of the tax. So, for Abalo, things were alright. It was warm and dry inside the cave. There were plenty of sheanuts to eat, and Obal-lim could look after the young child she left at home.

At nightfall, it was still raining. The large raindrops fell like pieces of stones. It rained on and on and on like the quarrelling of women. When finally it stopped at about midnight, I was already born. My cries slashed the roof of the cave as I inhaled the thick foul air. Mosquitoes, fleas and a thousand little insects sucked my infant blood like elders sucking *lacol* beer at a funeral, such that when I was taken home, my skin was rough like the tongue of an ox, and itchy like scabies.

All these were told me by my maternal grandfather, Sergeant Otto Bwangomoi, after I had grown up into a little boy. He had come home on a short leave from *Keya,* King's African Rifles, when I was born, and he had written down the name of the day, the moon and the year, and had kept the book in a small wooden box. Unfortunately, when I began to smoke, I used leaves from the book to wrap my *abugwe,* tobacco, and now I cannot tell the exact date on which I was born. But I suppose it does not really matter, does it?

When Sergeant came home again on another short leave, I had grown up into a strong little boy. Oh! I remember how all the children were extremely excited because he had brought each one of us a small gift. He brought me a red *lacomi,* frontkerchief, which I kept in a pot in my mother's hut. I would look in on it before going out to tend goats in the pastures to see if it was still there, and I would repeat the ritual when I brought the goats home in the evening.

When Sergeant was on leave we kept very clean. For after bringing goats home in the evenings, we would all get into the rocky stream and have a thorough bath with the carbolic soap he brought us. We brushed the sides of our feet so that they sparkled as we walked back home. Then we would gather around the old man and shower him with questions.

"Sergeant, where do you live?"

"I live in the *dunia* of the Abas people. It is a very long way from here."

"And what do the Abas people look like?"

"The Abas are tall, *lakini* they have *nguvu sana.* In battles, they never run away. I tell you, in that war of Gondar town, even women and children like you, had guns or pistols, or *kisu* or *panga* or grenades. Everyone was armed with a bayonet or some other weapon for fighting."

The old sergeant spoke as if to his fellow soldiers. We could not follow what he was talking about, but it was very fascinating to listen to him. He could pause briefly to light his

4

brass-rimmed pipe, and give us a chance to rush in a question. And if you asked him about something you did not know, he would reply using a lot of other words you did not understand. The game was like the singing of *tutu* birds, one after the other.

"Sergeant, what is Gondar?"

"Gondar is a big town, a big village in the Abasland where we fought the eighth battle. Captain John Embi, Brigadier James Koon, Lieutenant Mufuleny, Sergeant Edwardi Sayi, and Sergeant-Major Marijan. All of the Third Battalion, King's African Rifles. Number 2218, Corporal Aduce; Number 2217 Corporal Onyutta; and I, Number 2216. We fought side by side. We hit Gondar *kabisa!*"

"What is *bunduki?*"

"*Bunduki* is a bullet, a bullet is a trigger. It has inside it *risasi* as big as your little finger. It is red death, child. One type is called bren-gun, then there is a bomb, and this is different from machine-gun because machine-gun is different from bomb."

If we asked him too many questions, he did not like it. When too many children wanted to ask him questions all at once, he lined us up in threes and commanded us and we would march and counter-march while singing either:

> *Obong kara lwor*
> *Obong kara lwor*
> *Muno otara tyeko dano do*
> *Mh, mh Obong kara lwor* . . . . .

Or:

> *Ito Got Alur muloyo lacek*
> *Ngat ma ito pe*
> *Kiri-ni-kijing* . . . . .

Or:

> *Funga safari*
> *Funga safari*
> *Funga safari*
> *Funga safari*
> *Funga safari, captain*
> *Funga safari* . . . . .

5

The old man liked the company of children. He disliked grown-ups because they never allowed him to speak as long and as much as he wanted to. We loved him dearly because he was a great talker, and while he was at home, we were never caned very much. Any child under threat of the cane would seek refuge in his house.

* * * *

My father had thirty-five goats which he bought from Karamoja. They were fat, white Karamoja goats. He did not want them to mingle with the thin, sickly goats of his brother. So he selected a special herdsboy; the bull of youth, Atuk, to look after his goats.

I had grown up into a youthful boy when I began to tend the goats. My father would not allow me to spend my tender years in the grazing fields, tending animals, because, he believed, this would prevent me from growing up into a tall, big man.

The herdsboys from the homestead of Latigo Not-kai on the other side of the stream were always very hostile towards us. They often sent provocative messages that whenever we met, there could be a big fight. But we were also ready for them. One day, after we had taken the goats to drink water at the stream, we went to inspect our *wino* set under a big *kituba* tree by the stream. Everything was in chaos. Some of the *wino* had been pulled up, others broken or entangled. The birds that had been trapped in some of them were plucked away... the whole place was so full of bird feathers that you would think some *ogwang,* wild cat, had visited the *wino*. We spread out to search for the enemies' footprints. Oryem saw them, they were like spoors of a herd of elephants that had raided millet fields.

We followed the footmarks up to the mouth of the forest before we lost them. We looked further around in vain. We started returning to the *kituba* tree, feeling bitterly disappointed for failing to find the provokers.

"I know it is the boys from the other side of the stream."

"It is them alright. Who else could have done such an offensive thing? If we had found them today, they would have had a taste of our manliness."

"I would very much have liked to meet them. What they have done is like fondling our testicles. I would rather we followed them further. This *pobo* twigged cane of mine should not wither before it is used."

The boys dared, vowed, and cursed as they staged mock-attacks by striking great blows on the ground and nearby trees with their canes. Some of them, however, were mere hyenas. Only very few were brave, and these did not brag, knowing well that a roaring lion does not kill a prey. So they left the bragging to those we referred to as "the fire side praters".

We gathered to rest under the big tree and at the same time repair and reset the bird-traps.

"These boys are really hard-headed. When we meet them next time, it doesn't matter where, I am prepared to fight them to death, even single-handedly."

These were words from the mouth of Otto Luru. He was the oldest and biggest among us, extremely loud-mouthed, strongly built; a young bull to all appearances. Unfortunately, he was only mouth, as his words were never matched with deeds. He was extremely faint-hearted.

While we were still vowing, bragging, and cursing, something shook the branches of the tree under which we were. We looked up to see what it was and our eyes met with sand and some kind of water which made our eyes smart, though it did not have a salty taste, or smell.

We all ran down to the stream. Those who had sand in their eyes, opened them wide under the water. Those whose eyes were smarting washed them. Then we returned to the tree, stones gathered on our chests.

We started stoning the boys up the tree as if we were stoning grey monkeys.

The screams in the *kituba* tree were like the yells of chickens whose pen was being raided by *ogwang* at night. I sent a stone

7

powerfully and it hit something which sounded like a human chest. I felt the thud quite clearly and saw something like blood dripping from the tree. The wailing in the treee now sounded like *odir* insects shrilling during the mating period. One of the boys broke off with a branch and came tumbling down, head first. I was afraid he was the one I had hit and that he was now dying! It was a good thing to be manly, but then, there were the white man's laws! I could not call out my *mwoc*. My mouth suddenly dried up. Cold fear gripped me, my heart started racing and aching. . . .

But I was deceived! I had hit a branch of the tree and the red liiquid I saw dripping was not human blood but *kituba* sap!

As soon as the boy who had fallen down got up, he lashed at Otto Luru on the thigh, and Otto took off at an unbelievable speed! The rest of the Bol-kol boys climbed down the tree quickly and charged at us as fiercely as the soldiers in the battle of Gondar town which Sergeant Otto Bwangomoi used to tell us about.

On our side, there were now only Okello Todwong, Oryem Dako-kali, Pido Dako-kolo-tyeni and myself. As we were still trying to organize ourselves for defence, Oryem was surprised by a slashing pain of a *pobo* cane on the ear. Making as if to cry, and shouting his *mwoc* at the same time in pain and fury, the boy took off, his heels almost knocking against his buttocks! There were now only three of us left to face the enemies.

The Bol-kol boys advanced towards us like deeply wounded she-buffaloes.

One of them raised his *pobo* cane to hit Pido but I hit him on the elbow before he could do so. His cane fell down. Todwong immediately lashed him with his forked cane on the back. The boy urged his legs to take him quickly away from the battle front.

As soon as his friends saw that he was fleeing, they too urged their legs to save them from us. They headed for the stream, with us in the hot pursuit, as we called out our *mwoc* names:

"Your-wife-jumped-over-you-in-the-morning!"

"*Oryang*-thorn-tore-your-earlobe!"

"You-disturbed-*ten*-in-your-mother-in-law's hut!"

We shouted our *mwoc* but with some reservation for the enemies had not yet been completely defeated. .

The Bol-kol boys returned from the stream more determined than before. They came at us, thirsting for blood. They had now thrown away canes and acquired bamboo clubs. We also had to look for more reliable weapons with which to protect ourselves. We kept close together.

One of the aggressors hit his foot against a stump and the nail of the big toe came off and blood started squirting like a spring of water! A friend of his stopped to help him away. The three remaining advanced on us in a blind fury.

Todwong hurled his club and it landed right on the neck of the leading attacker. The fellow fell down and one of his companions bent down to give him a helping hand. The one remaining, sensing defeat, tried to retreat. But before he could run away, I sent my club between his legs, and he fell down heavily. I shouted my *mwoc* in excitement:

Atuk, *Otuk ruk!*

You disturbed *ten*

In your mother-in-law's hut!

We now called out our *mwoc* names loudly for indeed we had won the fight and our enemies were routed and put to flight. We drove their animals far away and scattered them all over the place. This was for *nyong!*

We went back to our goats which we had left grazing and started herding them homeward for the sun was beginning to disappear. As we neared our homestead, we could hear faintly some low moans. We thought, "Ah, that must be Otto Luru and Oryem still crying!" We promised to lash the two cowards with words for running away from the fight like women. That would be the following day, anyway, for we were too hungry just then for such a thing.

I entered my mother's hut. She was not in. I checked the

9

place where she usually kept food for me. There was nothing. I searched everywhere in the hut. Every place was dry and empty, I placed my right foot above the cooking place, it was cold. There had been no cooking today! I went out behind the hut to pass water. There was a fresh mound of brown soil, encircled with reeds! A new grave! Whose?! Nobody was ill when I left home this morning!

I decided to look for mother around the homestead, to give me something to eat, for the hunger in my stomach was now like a hundred rats gnawing at my inside! There was a gathering in Obal-lim's house. When I got within earshot, I heard voices coming from inside.

"But who? Who will look after my children? Who will look after them? Okeca, my son, what an unfortunate child you are!"

Obal-lim's voice answered mother's:

"Woman, stop talking that way! Are there no more men in this clan you mean? It is not nice at all to hear you say such a thing!"

Sergeant Otto's voice came out:

"Let her mourn. It is the pain of death making her utter such things. Death is very painful. It burns like fire."

"No! I don't want to hear her say such a thing again. If some stranger heard her saying such a thing, it would not be good at all!"

"Brother, you can say what you want. We shall see. We shall see if you will look after my children...."

"Do not answer Obal-lim back; do not even pay any attention to what he says. You just mourn. . . ."

"Okeca Ladwong. . . my child, Komakech! What is delaying you today? Has anything bad happened to you, my son, or to the animals...?"

I stood outside as if my feet had suddenly grown roots! I then uprooted myself and moved slowly and stood just by the door side where I could not be seen from inside. My knees were knocking against each other, but not with hunger – the hunger had vanished. I could hear the violent thuds of my heart against my chest, and the lungs lunged at each other like enraged wrestlers. My throat dried up and hot tears ran freely down my face.

I took a peep inside: mother was wearing a dress I had never seen before and her head was tied with some red band – *cola*! Her eyes were red like embers in the cooking place; her hands were tied together with a rope used for tethering the stubborn billy goat and two women on either side of her held her by the chest.

I felt a cold sweat drench me slowly as fear washed through my stomach, and surged up through my chest, my throat, and mouth. It spread through my limbs into my head. I stood still, dumb, deaf and blind .... My mother's eye fell on me. She gave a heart-rending scream like a pig that had been stabbed at the death spot! She broke loose like a possessed person and threw off the two women holding her. Strong men had to hold her now.

"Abalo Muca, why do you behave like this? Stop behaving that way! You must behave like a grown-up, Aciro's mother!"

"Obal-lim, do you really think you will care for me?!"

"Muca, do not behave that way . . . ."

"My friend, you have a husband to look after your children and you .... That's your luck ... we cannot all be lucky on this earth, can we?"

True, the woman telling my mother not to behave that way had her husband who was alive and well. But Abalo Muca, Tyena-teda, a woman from Atyak Lwani, mother of Okeca Ladwong, You-disturbed-*ten*-in-your-mother-in-law's-hut, and his sister Acirokop, had become a widow; Ojok Lapok, White-teeth-make-us-laugh-in-this-world, had become the late! From now on, Okeca Ladwong was an orphan; he and his sister were now fatherless.

One morning many days later, when I was about to take goats out to graze, mother called me and told me I should not go out to tend the animals that day as it was the day my father's last funeral rites were going to be performed. I was excited

11

because I was going to escape the hunger herdsboys always went through and, of course, the fights with other herdsboys while out grazing animals.

A big bull was slaughtered. Beer was as plenty as that made for marriage celebrations. Indeed, the day was a mixture of pain and pleasure, sadness and happiness because some people enjoyed themselves thoroughly while others wept bitterly.

When people had eaten and drank enough to put them into a dancing mood, dance drums were brought out. People danced the funeral dance singing:

Fire rages at Layama
Fire rages at the valley of River Cumu
Everything is utterly, utterly burnt
Fire rages at the valley of River Cumu
If I could reach Death's homestead
I would light a long grass torch
I would burn everything there utterly, utterly
Like the fire that rages at the valley of River Cumu....!

True, if you could reach Death's homestead, you would destroy everything there completely. Unfortunately, Death's homestead is reached only through the grave!

Throughout the night, people drank, ate sang, danced and some even made love! The following day, father's two wives were given out, as the custom required, by the clan elders. My mother was handed over to Obal-lim, and my mother's co-wife was inherited by Jeremiya Nyako whose *mwoc* name was, He-who-leaked-out-a-murder-plan. My father's property was shared out among his brothers and other close relations in a way I did not follow.

One day after many days had passed, Obal-lim, who was now my second father, told me that I should look after my late father's goats well because they were my wealth and that one day they would help me pay bridewealth. And that was the end of my father: dead, buried, eaten, drunk, danced, sang, and forgotten.

I grew up into a strong young boy. Some of Obal-lim's sons

12

joined the *Keya* to go and fight Hilter. Otibi took over the herding of goats from me and Okeny and I started looking after Obal-lim's cattle.

CHAPTER TWO

"Rip kipi!

You girl in front of the other girls, look this way!

I will take you to live with me under the cool shadows of Ladwong Hill;

To eat shea butter;

To the land of ghee and milk and honey;

To live with me in peace and confort,

And to adorn your beautiful neck

With giraffe tail-hair necklaces...!"

I was the first man to "shoot" at the girl in front of the rest, such that even though my friends must have had their eyes on her too, they left her for me.

It was Saturday, the Market Day. The Paibona girls were walking in a single file, to the market at the palace of *Jago* Sub-chief Temceo Ajak. We the young men from the valley were also going to the market to socialise or, "to watch people," as we say.

That girl in front of the others was spotless. Tall but not too tall. Brown, yet not brown. Her skin was tender like the young grass shoot. It was so soft and tender as if she used Lux bathing soap. This must have been the case, for her brother had just come home on leave from the army.

She was leading the other girls to the market like a bull antelope leading others to the drinking place. She had draped her tender frame with a soft silky dress and on her crested crane neck was a single giraffe-tail hair necklace. Her hair was carefully combed and pressed, and on her head was balanced an *abino,* earthen jar, whose neck was like that of its carrier.

Faultlessly beautiful.

14

Spotlessly clean.

The leader of girls bore *abino*.

Cecilia Laliya, chief of girls!

"Rip kipi! Mine is the girl at the tail of the line! Girl, I shall take you to drink *oak lukulu* under the Ladwong Hill!"

"Carrier of a new basket, look at me, my love! If you are shy, you will miss a good man for a husband!"

"Mine is the girl in the middle of the line! Girl, I will take you with me to enjoy cow butter, to drink the cold water from the Ladwong Hill, the water that never dries up in the dry season!"

"Rip kipi! I am dying with love for the girl in front of the girl in the middle of the line!"

In a short while, we were all in twos. Each man with his own girl, except Otto Luru who had branched off a bit in the grass for a long call, just before we saw the Paibona girls around the corner. Soon we were wooing in earnest:

"I say, daughter of my mother-in-law, my love for you is very, very strong indeed. I want you to be my first wife, the senior wife, the woman on whose finger I will put a wedding ring!"

"I do not love you."

"Why do you not love me? Am I not fit to be your husband, or what reasons have you?"

Your girl would remain silent. You would repeat the same question three or four times, but the daughter of your mother-in-law would stubbornly remain silent. To make her speak, you firmly held her arm so that blood could not flow freely. She would then scream, "Let go my arm, you stranger man! You hold my arm and what if something harmful happens to me?"

The young man would answer in anger, for it is only sorcerers that can harm if they touch you:

"Will you stop insulting me, you little girl! Do not dare abuse me again! Do you think I am a sorcerer? What sharp tongue you seem to have!"

"Do you have to hold a girl's arm when you love her? Can I not hear you if you do not hold my arm so powerfully?"

15

"But I asked you a question several times and you kept silent as if you had some soil in your mouth that you feared might flow out if you opened your mouth to talk!"

"I have already told you that I do not want you. What more do you want to hear from me? There is no reason for not being in love with you, that's all."

"Does any woman on earth resist a man for no reason at all? Now you are going to the market, but are you going to do nothing there? Is it not perhaps that..."

The girl would hiss at you like an angry snake and say:

"Talk of abusing people! It is you, is it not, who is abusing me? Does any man who truly loves you not go to woo you from your father's homestead? Which man woos a girl on the way?"

The market was filled like a beer pot. Saturday. Some buyers had come from as far as Gulu; others had come on bicycles from far away Labwor-Omor. There were so many buyers and sellers at the market place that if you feared knocking against other people as you moved about, you better kept away from the place altogether.

The ground looked all reddish brown! There were cassava tubers cooked or raw with skin peeled off; sweet potatoes boiled or unskinned – they looked so unappetising! Honey attracted live bees which buzzed everywhere. Curdled and fresh milk, same price – a broad calabashful costing ten cents. Sugarcane tied in bundles of fifteen cents each. Shea butter, and sheanuts; fresh groundnuts just harvested, or fried and salted ones: simsim and *lamola* unprepared millet, millet grains and millet flour crushed and dried tobacco, cakes and earthen smoking pipes, fired earthen pots and dishes, ropes for penning goats and cattle, and for tying things on bicycle carriers, knives and spears and wooden bowls, wooden stools and wooden head-rests.... Everything was there in large quantities. You carefully chose what you wanted to buy, and rejected what you did not.

The noise from the market place, combined with the buzzing

16

of swarms of bees and houseflies, from afar sounded like noise from a great feast at a chief's palace.

Everything was there. Not only foodstuffs: men who were long past their peak but still bachelors would find spinsters also past their prime; married women with withered love for their husbands could find men who loved their wives less.... Young men who had lived away from home used the market-day to expose themselves. Market-day: Saturday! It was a hunting day and a day on which to be hunted.

"Man, when did you come home?"

"I arrived only yesterday, friend, and I am going back tomorrow...!"

"But listen, you pretty one. You must consider my marriage proposal now, because I have little time left before I go back. My short leave ends next week I want to go back with you to where I live. I want you to make up your mind now and not tomorrow because I want to make arrangements to marry you *kas kas*, without delay... I am ready from my feet to my head to marry you even tomorrow. I do not want *opuji* matter, therefore, stop *maneno maneno* of children. I want you for marriage this week!"

"But where do you live?"

"I live in Nairobi, Kenya. Far away from here. You go there by train. I am the headman of all the Railway *pagazi* in Nairobi; a very big job with a big pay."

"I have nothing to say against your proposal, but you must first come to my father's homestead."

"Now you go and inform your parents. I do not need from you any article like a bangle or a necklace or some lines of your waist-beads to show you love me; the words from your mouth are enough proof."

On that day, you must not do anything or go anywhere else. And if you had guests in your home, you must not leave them behind. They too must visit the market place. Saturday: the market-day: a unique social occasion. A day not to miss.

"My husband quarrels with me everyday. I am really unlucky

in marriage."

"Friend, you are lucky your husband only quarrels with you. Mine! He comes home drunk every night and beats me to kill. Ochan's father is a beast, not a human being."

"That's our lot, married women. Treated like slaves, not as properly married wives. I wish I could be lucky enough to find a man to elope with..."

"You are reminded all the time about the bride price. Now and again you hear. 'Do you think the thousands of shillings I paid on you was a small amount? Don't you realise I bought you with money I suffered to earn?' "

"We are mere property bought off the market stall. You know, I insisted my parents should not demand too much money on me, but in vain. Acoli parents these days seem to value money more than their daughters."

"As for me, if I could find a man who could be in a position to refund the bridewealth of Ochan's father on me, I would run away to him. Of course, I know I have children by my husband, but I am not willing to continue suffering at the hands of the man...."

The women talked loudly, for everyone to hear. Acoli women talk that way. Whenever our women are on the way to the market, or to fetch water or firewood, even when they are only two, they never talk only for each other's ears. They talk at the top of their voices for everybody who cares to listen. But today, Ochan's mother and her friend were talking loudly on purpose. They wanted married men with dwindled loves for their clumsy wives to hear them.

"I say, Ochan's mother, would you stop for a while, please?"

"Who's that, Nyaga, asking me to stop for a moment?"

"I do not know the man. I think he may be interested in you. You are always lucky with men."

"You man, I don't seem to know you. If my husband found me talking to you, it would be very bad indeed. Are you going to the market too?"

"Yes. How are you?"

"I am well. How's your home?"

"It is peaceful, and yours?"

"Ours is peaceful too except the usual headaches from men. But you better hurry and tell me what you want to tell me... I fear being seen talking to you here...."

"Listen, Ochan's mother, stop unnecessary fear. I have asked you to stop a while because it pains me very much to hear that such a beautiful woman like you is suffering so much at the hands of an ugly man like Ochan's father."

"It is true I am suffering very much, but what can I do about it? That is our lot, housewives."

"How about running away with me? I can refund Ochan's father's bride price on you any time, any day. I want you to leave your husband's home. Ochan's father is very poor indeed."

"But where do you live."

"I live in Kampala city. I am a prison sergeant. I do not want to delay with this matter because I have come home to look for a woman to marry. My wife did something very bad indeed. She eloped with an army sergeant, thinking soldiers earn more money than prison warders do. This is untrue, of course. So if you have no interest in me, let me know it now so that I continue my search among the women attending the market..."

There were so many people and items at the market. You walked with great care lest you put your foot in a pot of sour milk, or in a wooden bowl containing sheanut butter. Or you would tread on cooked potatoes, or break a calabash.

People walked or stood or sat down in groups. You did not shake hands with people you did not know very well; you might be touched with the deadly *lugaga,* poison! And moreover, it was now old-fashioned to shake hands when greeting someone. The modern way of greeting a person was waving your hand and shouting at him or her, *"Jambo!"*

Some young men had returned home briefly from as far away places as Gilgil in Kenya. There, they did not speak the

19

Acoli language. When they returned home after many years, they found it very difficult to speak Acoli without mixing it with some Swahili words. They too had come home to look for women to marry and go back with.

"*Lakini,* I shall take you with me to *dunia* of Gilgil. I can marry *wewe kas kas* without *kelele kidogo.* I have come home to marry you, *bas!* Speak, woman: will you come with me to Gilgil? I extend my right hand across the River Acaa, reaching out for you. I am not an *adui,* and I don't want *maneno ya mchezo.* I want your *majibu sasa!* Give me your bangle or a line of your waist-beads as an article of love."

"Can't you come first to my father's home?"

"Leave *yangu nakwisha. Nyumbani wapi?*"

"Eh?"

"Your home *wapi?*"

"Oh, our home is near the PWD works camp. The home of Antonio, the village headman...."

By two in the afternoon, only a few people remained in the market place: Some aged men selling ropes for tethering animals; sellers of dry fish, and of empty cans; grandmothers whose *oceyo* fruits had not sold because of their high prices. Young women had already left for home to go and cook for their families. As for young men, what was the point of their lingering about the market when there were no more girls around?

We escorted the Paibona girls up to the outskirts of their homestead. Cecilia took the opportunity to point out to me her mother's hut from among several others in her father's compound. There was no hint on her face, or voice, or words or actions to show the slightest sign of love for me, nor was there any to show that she didn't love me either.

She only kept repeating that she did not love me without giving any reason for it. But then, that is the way of all Acoli girls: they never say "yes" to a man. You have to read their "yes" in their "protest" behaviour. And again, a young Acoli woman can never accept a man on their very first meeting.

20

* * * *

One Sunday, there was an *orak* dance to celebrate the marriage of the son of Timotimo. Many people came to participate. Timotimo's son, Jakeo Onen, had married a sub-chief's sister, and Onen was not only the assistant chief for youth, but he was also extremely popular because of his good manners.

When the Palaro young men arrived with a brand new set of dance drums specially made for the occasion, Ting-dwilo Lapac played the solo drum, Olok Jok-daa-Lunebi, the two rhythm drums, and the well known drummer, Ajulino Bene-dato, beat the mother drum. The solo and the rhythm drums sang in harmony:

Tamam afonde! I have come back!

I have delayed *afonde,* but I have come back!

I have been marrying a woman, *afonde* I have been marrying.

Akello Kele, daughter of Patongo clan

Tamam afande, I have just arrive back....!

Ajulino palmed the mother drum and it boomed:

It is good you have come back!

It is good you have come back!

There's a big dance, there's a big dance!

It is good you have come back....!

And then Olinga leapt in the air and in an honeyed voice, called out the tune of the song, "The bridewealth is not there," like the *ogilo* bird at sunset. The young men, inspired and full of themselves, took up the tune and beating rhythmically on their dance half-gourds, each celebrated his own love life, chorusing:

I have no bridewealth

Where shall I find the cattle

With which to bring my love home?

The beautiful one, stop, wait for me,

Let me take you away even from your husband!

21

And I have no sister,
Where shall I gather the cattle from
With which to bring my woman home?
The beautiful one, stop, wait for me
Let me take you away even from your husband!

Shortage of wealth has treated me cruelly, oh
Whose cattle shall I raid
So that I may marry my woman with?
Let me take you away even from your husband!

And I have no father
Where will this young man find money
With which to pay the fornication fine?
You, woman, stop for me
Let me take you away even from your husband!

The bridewealth is not there
I will use the bridewealth of my uncle's daughter
To bring my girl, Kele, home
The beautiful one, stop, wait for me
Let me take you away even from your husband...!

Cecilia Laliya, sister of Otto, Laliya the chief of girls, was there in front of all the Paibona girls, leading the dancing beauties. She was wearing a nylon dance skirt, her breasts barely covered. The breasts were ripe like a pair of ripened *tugu* fruits and the tatooes on her back were like *olok* fruits. Her heels sparkled as she danced; her hair shone, black and thick but not bushy. Cecilia, stunningly beautiful! Whose daughter could compare with her!

On that day, we, the young men from the valley did not go to participate in the dance but to watch. Cecilia was there in the arena! She was dancing, challenging and provoking all! I beckoned her out of the arena so that we would converge a little. She obeyed. A perfumed scent she exuded filled my nostrils. The glowing sunset light made the healthy sweat

22

flowing freely on her smooth skin look like strings of glassy beads. She stood there, smiling, exposing teeth and a gap in the upper row of teeth. The teeth were white beyond compare! What a haunting beauty Cecilia's teeth were!

"How's it with you today? Why aren't you dancing today?" She ventured to ask me after seeing I could not bring myself to say anything to her. But could I answer her? Where could Okeca Ladwong get the voice with which to say anything to Cecilia when her beauty had dazzled and robbed him of words! Otto Luru had to come to my rescue:

"Today we have decided to come and feed our eyes on pretty ones like you."

"Okeca, you better tell me quickly what you have called me here for. I want to go back and dance," she said, dancing.

I gathered some male courage:

"I do not have much to say to you, Acil. I only want you to give me an article of yours to show that you have accepted me as your future husband. It is pointless accepting me without any proof."

"I have no article to give you."

"What about all those giraffe tail-hair necklaces round your neck?"

"They are not mine. . . I borrowed them from a friend for the dance. Anyway, what do you want them for...?"

I could see Cecilia's lurking, "yes", which is never mentioned by an Acoli young woman when she is being wooed. A young man has to read her "yes". Therefore, Laliya was not going to remove the necklaces from round her neck and hand them over to me herself. She had to feign unwillingness. So sooner or later, I would have to apply a little force to get the necklaces myself despite her little protest behaviour....

Just as I was about to take the necklaces from Cecilia's neck, a bull of a man, calling out his *mwoc* name and lulating in a terrifying manner, raced towards us from the arena, and buried his gleaming and very sharp dance axe in the ground very near my toe, demanding: "What are you saying to Cecilia?"

My friend. Pido, sensing trouble, ran to us:

"Ladwong, what is the fellow saying? If he wants to fight you, we are all ready to face him! We are ready for him!"

The fellow got so mad with fury that his eyes grew baleful. He wielded the axe and buried it in the ground between me and Pido.

"Who? Who among you, rats, wants to touch this axe? I will split his head right here and now! We are ready for him! What a death wish!"

Otto Luru took off towards the arena, shouting at the top of his voice. He was calling an imaginary Otori from our village to come to our aid.

"Otori! Otori! Come and help us! There is a bully of a man here!"

He then ran back towards us muttering:

"Does the fellow think there are no grown-ups here from our village? Let him wait... the Otoris are coming. You bully, do you think we do not have grown-up brothers? If you want to fight us, start it now! You want our sister and at the same time you want to fight her brothers! Don't you know Cecilia is from Paibona? What are you waiting for, standing there with your axe? Go ahead and split our heads with it! Otori and others are coming...."

The man's mouth dried up. He became confused.

"Go on then! If you want to kill Cecilia's brothers, go right ahead! But you will not escape the white man's law."

"I am sorry, very sorry indeed. I did not know your were Cecilia's brothers."

"Did you not know it? Kill us and you will see to whom you will pay the dowry on Laliya."

"Forgive me, brother-in-law... forgive me...."

In the arena, a fight broke out. The Bungatira young men were very strict on their sisters, and yet they wanted Tyenakaya girls from Alokolum.

We had to abandon Cecilia and run to the arena. The fighting young men were separated before blood was spilt.

Oryem Girawel whose *mwoc* name was, You-refused-to-return-the-bridewealth, and who was in-charge of the dance, climbed the drum post and soon there was silence. He addressed people:

"Listen, you young men! This dance is a dance for happiness. It is a marriage celebration dance. Why do you want to ruin it with a fight? You young men of today do not understand things. Who ever fought during a marriage celebration dance? Why do you want ill-luck to befall our son? If any of you is drunk, let him leave! If any of you wants to be a killer, let him go and join the army! That's where people are trained and paid to kill! This is a dancing arena, not a battlefield. He who starts a fight again will be shown the way to his father's homestead quickly! Dance in peace!"

There were loud cheers, drumming, yodelling, rattlings on the dance half-gourds... and dancing started afresh, with renewed vigour. But Acoli youth in any dance are always itchy like jiggers between toes. All the songs sang now were insulting and would make someone angry.

Young men were seen now openly challenging one another by pushing, pulling and even poking each others ribs, with their elbows. Soon another fight flared up. There was chaos everywhere in the arena. Oryem took away the drums and the dance came to an abrupt end. Young men could be seen chasing after girls like edible rats. How and where Cecilia Laliya, chief of girls, disappeared to, no one could tell.

25

CHAPTER THREE

When a boy grows up into a young man, he must be told all about the home. He must be acquainted with all the relations, their issues and he must be fully briefed on wealth matters, land issues, old feuds, money lent out and borrowed, etc. All should be made known to the young man because he will soon head the home.

Obal-lim had four sons and three daughters of his own. Together with my sister and I, his late brother's children, there were now nine of us in his charge. Onen and I were now old enough to marry, and were actually looking around for eligible girls. Ongiya was still young.

Two of Obal-lim's daughters had got married and their bridewealth was used by their brothers to acquire wives. Lakop, the third daughter, was in the process of getting married. Her suitor had already paid some money for her, but was told it was too little and that he should go and bring more money.

Obal-lim was a very mean and miserly man indeed. He would never allow any money to get out of his hands easily but he would go to any lengths to get money into his hands. His sons who were now married did not find it easy to obtain money from him for dowry. Obal-lim released the money very reluctantly only after some bitter quarrels that threatened to break up the family. Perhaps that was what had brought ill-health to his daughters-in-law. The young women's skins were always dry, and their lips cracked even during the rainy season, and had to be softened constantly with shea butter.

One day I called on Obal-lim, who was now my second father. He was with his brother-in-law, Obigu, whose *mwoc* name was, The-billy-goat's testicles. They were both drinking *lacoi* beer. When I called out, *hodi,* it was Obal-lim who answered, *karibu,* come in.

"Come in, son. But what is the matter today? You used to fear coming to talk to me.... The-billy-goat's-testicles, this is the son of my late brother, White-teeth-make-us-laugh-in-this-world. He is the only son he left in this world."

"So this is the son of my friend! Good, son, May you have good health. Death is no good. Oh, your father, Ojok Lapok. It-is-white-teeth-that-make-us-laugh-on-earth, was a very good friend of mine. Very good indeed. Well, child, go ahead and talk your father."

"I have come, father, because I think I am now an old enough person. And besides, there is something I would like us to talk about..."

"Something you want us to talk about? What is this something you want us to talk about now? Don't you think if there is something for us two to talk about, it should be me to ask you to come to me? I don't want unnecessary headaches."

"Don't talk to the child that way, *ladit.* The child has done no wrong by coming to you. If he does not come to you, who do you expect him to go and seek advice from when he wants to find out something?"

"My brother-in-law, you are a guest here and do not know what goes on in this homestead. The children in this home are very troublesome. I don't have time to waste on listening to nonsense!"

"Brother, the young rhino bull compares the size of its spoor with that of its father, and when the sizes are more or less equal, it challenges the father for the supremacy of the herd. A time comes when the son asserts his independence from his father's authority and demands to be treated as an adult. You don't have to be told that, do you?"

I thought that the two elders did not quite get right what I was trying to get at, so I changed the approach.

"I have no ill-intention in coming here, my elders. My real

father is dead, and we all know that is the way of this world. Obal-lim is now my father as he inherited my mother according to custom. Now that I am grown up, I feel I have a right to know all about this homestead. Obal-lim has never sat me down before him to brief me about these things. What shall I do if I grew up wild like grass in the old field?"

Obal-lim shouted his *mwoc:*

Your tobacco bag is empty

You provoked a mamba

In the hole of *mwoc*

A black billy goat has broken the water pot!

This outburst took Obigu and me with complete surprise.

"What is it, Obal-lim? What is it now?"

"Nothing, brother-in-law. I have only intoned my *mwoc.*"

"Obal-lim, husband of my sister, when one is an elder, one should not behave the way you have done just now. You are the head of this household and should not talk to a child like that. If an elder behaves the way you are doing, children will copy you. Listen, in-law, when we talk of bringing up children, we do not merely mean giving them enough food to eat. It means more than that. This child has come to you meekly to find out something, why don't you give him a chance to do so? The child's father is dead. You are now his father."

"In-law, you have been wrong here...."

Father got up as if something had stung him in the bottom. He staggered towards his bedroom, talking and belching, although I thought he was not that drunk.

"I do not want any stupid utterances here. Do you think you know more about things in this home than I do? Money! Did anybody's father die and leave me any money to look after? I don't want to hear any more foolish words from anybody's mouth. I do not want my wife to be troubled. Does this child not have a sister to marry off and get bridewealth?"

"Don't try to shield yourself behind a quarrel. You are wrong in this matter, Obal-lim!"

"Why don't you go and marry for him a wife then?"

"Do you think that if this was my nephew I could not have taken him away with me immediately and married him a wife? What an irresponsibility! Do you think when my nephew Ongiya is ready to marry and you are unwilling to give him money to marry with, I will not come to his aid?"

This is it, Okeca Ladwong, Atuk, *Otuk ruk!* You-disturbed-*ten*-in-your-mother-in-law's-hut! What else do I still want to hear from him? What more is there for me to be told in order to realise that I am alone in this world? That I should wait for my sister to get married so that I may use her brideprice to marry with! But what was Aciro, my sister?

A mere seven-year old! To make matters worse, young men these days preferred girls who had read books. Worse still, my sister was sickly. Her stomach was swollen, and she was only a bag of bones, with a large head like a toadpole in the Oitino stream. All kinds of diseases had fallen deeply in love with Aciro: sore-eyes, ulcers, scabies... all sorts of illnesses were competing for my sister's hand. If these diseases were some rich young men, I would have married my sister off to one of them and used the money to marry Cecilia Laliya! Now what was I to do in order to obtain money for Laliya's dowry? I was not going to remain a bachelor until my sister got married.

A girl should get married when she has just shot up, her breasts still sitting erect on her chest. And this moment came only once in the life of a young woman. Cecilia was like this now. She was at the peak of her prime. At this moment she was like the full blown *polok* flower, fragrant and lovely to behold. Bees and other insects were rushing to her: some to steal the honey, others merely to eat away the flower and leaves. But unlike many young beautiful women whose beauty dazzles the eyes, Cecilia Laliya had selected only one young man, Atuk, *Otuk ruk* to eat her honey. As proof of her strong love for me, she had given me three strings of her waist-beads, three bangles, and had of course, paid me a night visit in my *otogo,* bachelor's hut. I must marry Cecilia soon. Now! But where could I steal the money with which to marry her?!

CHAPTER FOUR

I was till young able-bodied, and physically strong. I did not fear working as a labourer, carrying murram for road repairs with the PWD, Public Works Department. Carrying murram in a basin on my head the whole day could not be impossible work for me. It was better than being jobless anyway, it was also much, much better than earning money only once in a year from growing cotton. And I feared I would soon be drafted into *luroni,* the conscript labour system just introduced by the white man's government. If that happened to me, my entire cotton crop of the season could get ruined in the fields. This was very common now. Able-bodied young men were taken away to go and work for months leaving at home their young wives and children and aged parents with no one to look after them! Yes, I should join the PWD to avoid being enlisted into the hated *luroni.*

But how much could I earn from PWD in one year? And how long could it take me to save one thousand shillings with which to marry?

I went to Cimayo Lakidi, son of our sub-chief, who was on school holiday, to work it out for me. This was what he came up with: I would be paid a wage of eighteen shillings per month. In a year I could earn two hundred and sixteen shillings.

He also added up the amount of money I could be paying out: Poll Tax and Labour Tax would add up to twenty-eight shillings.

He explained to me that I would have a balance of one hundred and eighty-eight shillings. But I would also need to spend some money on myself. What would Cecilia think of me if I did not dress up well? She might even change her mind about marrying me. I should also buy dresses for mother and sister because they were now under my charge. In total, I would spend in a year, eighty-eight shillings on mother, sister and myself. I would be left with one hundred shillings to save towards the dowry. To save one thousand shillings to marry Cecilia with, I would have to work for ten years.

Ten years! Would I still be young in ten years' time? Would Cecilia still be waiting for me? Could her brothers, who wanted her bridewealth to marry with, allow her to remain single for ten years?

No, I decided, PWD was out for me! What then? Sooner or later I might be drafted into *luroni* because the conscription had now been intensified. Gulu-Pakwach road was being built and the white government urgently needed more than three hundred able-bodied men for labour. There were also a number of buildings being put up in the new town of Gulu. Because of very low wages paid to workers, it was very difficult to get people to work at the building sites. And there were many young men streaming to the Bananaland to go and work there because, it was said, wages there were very high. The Baganda had refused to work as labourers unless wages were increased. As a result, a manual worker there was now earning thirty shillings every month.

I knew of many people whose sons had left home for unknown places and returned home in less than ten years, looking healthy and well dressed. What could stop me from venturing into the unknown as well? I was now a man. I could look for myself. And if I had to save mother and sister from the suffering they were going through now, I had to be adventurous. I must get money because the world of today was a world of money.

If you did not have money, you were a nobody. Those who were rich were the happy lot. It seemed that happiness was acquired not through physical strength and bravely but with money.

I related all these thoughts in my head to mother, and she too agreed with me, adding that if I did not do so, our suffering would never end. But I could not leave home immediately. I had to make some provisions for mother and sister.

I put two large fields under sweet potatoes, and one acre under cassava. Simsim, groundnuts and finger-millet were harvested and stored in large stores.

These days if you had no sister, you went to Bananaland to look for money to marry with. There was no more recruitment into the *Keya* because the big war against Hitler had come to an end with Hitler's defeat.

While mother was busy frying groundnuts for me to eat on my long safari, I went around the village collecting whatever money was still owed my late father. It was said that the only meal you could take with you on any long journey without fearing it going bad was money. I managed to get twenty shillings. Earlier, mother had managed to collect fifty shillings. That meant I had seventy shillings.

I then travelled the length and breadth of Ladwong villages, biding my friends and relatives goodbye, explaining to them the reason why I had decided to leave home and venture into the unknown world. I requested them to do me a favour by helping my mother occasionally by digging for her. The young men of our village understood my situation and sympathised with me. They promised to help mother as much as they could during my absence. They gave me presents of chickens to be slaughtered and prepared for me to eat before my journey.

Finally, I pleaded with Onen, son of Obal-lim, to make sure Cecilia did not misbehave with other young men in the village. She should wait for me patiently until I came back to marry her. The men who went to fight in the *Keya* against Hitler came back only to find their wives had either run away with other men or had had children by men who had remained at home. If married women could do that, what about Cecilia over whom I had no control yet! She was a buffalo in the hunting ground for the brave and skilful hunters. However, Onen promised to use all his persuasive skills to make her wait for me.

In the evening after we had had the parting meal, mother and I sat silently, both lost in thought. Both of us wanted me to leave home, but we wondered how mother would manage without me, and how I would fare in Bananaland.

"Mother, I have to leave home tomorrow. Look after Acirokop well. I shall go and return and find you both well."

"Go, my son. May you travel well and safely, stay there well and return well here. Nothing will harm you, son, for my heart is clean. I am not a cheat. Nobody's ill-wish will bring harm to you. I will look after your sister well. But my son, Komakech, you must not stay away too long. Don't go and disappear in the banana plantations."

"I'll not be lost there, mother. I will always remember you, my sister and home. I will not stay away too long. I am only going to look for money to come back and marry. I cannot remain a bachelor until Aciro gets married...."

"Do not go there and listen to other people's bad advice. It is poverty taking you away from your home, mother and sister. You are poor, your mother is poor, your sister is poor, and you come from a poor home. Do not go to Bananaland and start behaving like some rich man's brother."

"I know that, mother, I know it too well. I will go and live there as a person from a poor family. I will always remember the advice you have given me."

"Obal-lim is there alright. He inherited me and I now call him my husband. But he is my husband only in name. You are now my husband, son...."

Mother's words were loaded with suffering, pain and sadness. You could hear the pathos in the words she uttered as clearly as you could hear conceit in a person's voice. She advised me that I should lead an honest life while in Bananaland, and also revealed to me a lot of clan matters and secrets for the first time. She told me how my father had met his death: it was planned by his clansmen who offered him poison in drinks.... She told me so many other things that I cannot tell you here because some of them were top clan secrets, and they were so many that if all of them had to be written down, they would form a complete book that might be called: The Tragedy of a Family.

Mother and I talked until cock-crow, when she told me to go and get some sleep before setting off for the unknown land.

Before sunrise, I went to my maternal uncles who spat on me their blessings. They all wished me well, saying that nothing harmful should never cross my path. On the way back, I took the opportunity to go and bid Cecilia goodbye. Unfortunately, she had gone to visit her maternal grandmother at Bura.

In the afternoon, a bus left with us from Ajulu for Gulu town, a journey of fifteen miles. From there, another bus would take me to the famous city, Kampala, to search for money to marry Cecilia Laliya: Cecilia, daughter of Gurucenycio Obiya of Paibona.

* * * *

Atuk, *Otuk ruk!*
You disturb *ten*
In your mother-in-law's hut
Your eyes are dark
Because you do not want to share
The carcass of the cow
A thief dies in silence
However hard he is hit!

It is I, Atuk, still talking. It is my white teeth that still make me laugh in this world. If it was not for the white of my teeth, suffering would have stopped me from laughing.

I come from Patiko:
We are lions
We are a dish of okra
A little dish of okra
Finishes a whole *kwon.*

We are softeners
We cool you off
However fierce you may be
We are lions
We of Patiko are hot
Hot like pepper
We are itchy!

There was no clansman willing and ready to marry me a wife. I was like a pauper, *lapang-cla*. You may liken me to one of the homeless that roamed the streets of our big towns.

My mother comes from Atyak Lwani. But mother's people too had refused to marry me Cecilia Laliya.

Kinship is not something sung about, not something written in newspapers, not something paid lip-service to. Kinship is seen in action, by helping poor and needy relatives, seen in visiting sick kinsmen, attending funerals of departed relations.... Rich kinsmen should marry wives for their poor kin....

The Gulu to Atura bus used to travel every Monday and Thursday. The Monday bus left Gulu town very early in the morning. Travellers from distant places had, therefore, to spend the night at the bus station in order to get tickets for there were very many intending travellers. People going to Atura and Kampala were so many that if you did not spend the night at the Gulu bus station, you could not travel.

There were numerous women travelling to Kampala. Many were going to replace their co-wives who would come back and live at home for a while, a few were going to join their husbands who had been living alone, a number were eloping, others had come home to give birth and were now taking babies to their fathers, and several were old women going to visit their sons and daughters working in Bananaland. There was one woman who was in a very expensive looking dress although she looked quite old. People were whispering that she had some pieces of land in Kampala.

Those in school could easily be distinguished by their beautiful boxes and you could hear them speaking in English because educated Acoli boys and girls do not like speaking in their language when they are together, they want to show off their education! The boys wore their respective school uniforms: those wearing the green stocking and green coats with crested crane on the pocket were the Makerere boys; those in green and white stockings were students at Mbarara Teachers Training College in the land of the Banyankole; in white pullovers with red necks were Budo boys whose coats were black with a red lion on the chest bockets. Kisubi boys had black coats but with vultures perched on the chest; and the Mwiri boys had a jumping leopard on their coat pockets.

There were also many girls going to schools in far away places. They looked quite different from the girls in Ladwong village. They used white handkerchiefs to regularly wipe their beautiful lips.

Other travelling young men were not schoolboys. They were young village men going to Bananaland to seek work in order to earn money for bridewealth. They were wearing only *dura*, loin-cloths, their luggage slung on their clubs. Atuk, *Otuk ruk*, was one of them. They were all quiet because they did not know what lay ahead of them, where they were going to, while the other travellers talked excitedly.

At the ticket booking office, if you had a weak chest you would not manage to get a ticket. You had to press, shove, squeeze, push and pull people crowded on your way, shouting your *mwoc* as you do so, in order to get to the bus conductor. If you were the gentle or shy type, you could never get a ticket.

After I had booked my ticket, I entered the bus. To my surprise, I found all the schoolboys and schoolgirls already sitted! How did they get tickets? This made me think that getting tickets did not depend only on physical strength, for these schoolboys would never have got tickets at all.

When we were all sitted, the bus driver entered the bus, started the engine and sounded the horn to warn passengers that the bus was about to take off. Soon the bus started moving away, slowly. There were shouts of farewell:

"Safe journey...."

"Stay well..."

"Go and greet Sergeant Omac, Corporal Lacim...."

"Listen, Okello, tell father to write me a letter...."

"Please, don't forget to keep a watchful eye on my girl, Aryemo..."

The bus was now gathering speed as it moved out of the bus station.

"Gulu town, farewell...."

It was only Okeca Ladwong who had no one to see him off at the station!

I pushed my head out of the bus window near my seat. The Ajulu and Kijuu Hills and their brother Ladwong Hill started moving further and further into the distance and disappearing slowly as if they were sinking into some big holes in the ground:

Hills of our homeland, when shall I see you again?
Gulu, my hometown, when shall I return to you?
Friends, when shall we dance together again?
Mother, when shall I see you again?
Sister, Acirokop, my future wealth, when shall I again give you a brotherly piece of advice?
Cecilia, my beloved one, Laliya chief of girls,
When shall I see you and that beautiful *kere* gap in your upper teeth-row again?

I heard someone telling me like in a dream:

"You, young man! Do not put your head out of the bus window. Another vehicle travelling in the opposite direction may do you some harm."

Another voice said: "And what is the man crying for? Such a big man still cries for food left at the bottom of his mother's cooking pot like a child!"

I touched my cheek. It was wet with tears. I brushed the tears off with the back of my right arm and my eyes started smarting because of the sweat on my arm.

37

One schoolgirl was sitting beside me. She was reading a large newspaper, the type read by the white and educated people in Gulu. Her eyes were piercing like those of a white woman. When she looked at you, it was straight in the eyes, no shyness at all! She talked to you as if she was talking to a fellow girl and not a man!

"My friend, where are you going to?"

For sometime I could not answer her because I thought she had asked, "You man who cries without any apparent reason, where are you going to?" But I realised that if I did not say something quickly to her, people on the bus were going to start laughing at me.

"Well, I am going to Kampala."

"What are you going to do in Kampala?"

"Why do you want to know what I am going to do in Kampala?"

"Well, I just want to know what is taking you to Kampala, that's all."

"What about you, what are you going to do in Kampala"

"I am going to read... I am in a school there."

"If I told you what I am going to do in Kampala, in what way would it benefit you? Anyway, if you must know, I am going to Kampala to do nothing in particular."

Everybody in the bus burst into laughter. Her friend who was sitting just behind us and reading another large newspaper asked me:

"Are you really going to Kampala to do nothing?"

All the passengers were all ears and eyes on me. One man said: "Man how can you let mere girls defeat you in an argument?" Another one said: "The man is still a child that's why he was crying when we left Gulu town."

That I could be defeated by girls in an argument! I challenged the girl:

"Tell me: why, when men are wooing you girls, you keep telling them, 'I don't love you... I don't know why... There is no reason for it'... Is it perhaps to fool us men? Tell me! Even you, the educated ones, behave in the same way as the uneducated ones."

Everybody burst into hearty laughter.

We reached Atura at one o'clock in the afternoon because the bus broke down several times. The place was so full of people that there was hardly a place for one to stand. Many young men were going back home from Bananaland: Acoli people from Kitgum and from Gulu; the Madi from Moyo and from Pakele; the Lugbara, the Alur, the Jonam and the Langi had just been brought here by the steamer from the other side of Atura waters. They were all on their way home.

Everyone returning home had a small wooden box, a new blanket, a kettle and a saucepan. Most of them had brown shoes that cost nineteen shillings and ninety cents a pair. However, most of those shoes were not worn but carried in the hands, and those worn were worn without socks or stockings.

All the Acoli were represented here. You could tell this from the various Acoli accents being spoken. But the young men were now speaking the language and mixing it with some words from Swahili and Luganda. Although they were speaking in different Acoli variants, they were all speaking about the same thing – marriage.

"I am going back home to live in the village to marry a wife because I have now got the money to pay the dowry. I will go and dance the orak dance without any worry now because I have got enough money to marry with."

"I say! Which place in Acoliland do you come from?"

"I am from Patiko."

"Which clan in Patiko; Pugwenyi or Paraya?"

"I am a Pacua."

"Where are you going to; I can see you are leaving home?"

"I am going to where you are coming from."

"Do you know where I am coming from, Kampala a big town in Bananaland? I have spent there five years. I had gone there to search for money to marry with. And now that I have got it. I am going back home to marry."

"Are there some Patiko young men going back home too? *Mingi sana.* Here are all the clans of Acoli. Do you see that young man in a pair of khaki shorts, carrying a knife? He is from Patiko."

It was Opira, son of Can-dono, his real home was Paico but he was brought up by his maternal uncle in Ajulu. I knew him very well.

"Opira!"

"Yes, it is me. Oh, Ladwong, it is you, isn't it? You-disturbed-*ten*-in-your-mother-in-law's-hut!"

"You-filled-your-stomach-with-*oba*-animal-gravy!"

"Your eyes are dark for you want to eat alone!"

"The man in *giliri* animal skin broke a weighing scale!"

"A thief never cries in pain however hard he is boxed!"

"*Giliri* animal meat on the weighing scale!"

"Ladwong, Okeca, is this really you?"

"Opira, my brother, it is me."

"Where are you going to, friend?"

"I am going to the place you are coming from, man."

"Kololo is well. You will find there Obina... Obina son of... There are very many Acoli people in Kololo Number 66... Man, how's home?"

"Home is well, but some old ones have..."

"Don't bother me about the death of old people,... Is Akello still unmarried?"

"She is rumoured to have..."

"Lapyem Pirimon...? I forget her name... What's the girl's name?"

"Adokorac, you mean? A man who wanted to marry her took little money and was told to go back and bring more money."

"What about her younger sister, Amayo?"

"Amayo is already a mother, man."

"And what about Cecilia Laliya?"

"Laliya is mine, my friend; didn't you know that?"

"Ah! Ah! Ah! I was only teasing you, man. But tell me, are

there still some free girls for me to marry?"

The bus bound for Gulu started moving away from the station slowly.

"Go well, my friend. Greet mother, greet Laliya, greet everybody at home."

"You travel well too, to Kampala. Here, Ladwong, take this knife to protect yourself with. Obina is there. You will find him at Kololo!"

I tried to find out the name of Obina's father, but Opira could not remember it and he kept repeating: "The son of... the son of..." only. On the Gulu bus, a happy song broke out as the bus gathered speed, and so I never learnt the name of Obina's father.

The water at Atura was very wide, flowing to Miciri, Egypt, slowly, lazily. It flowed gently, quietly, uttering no threats of "come and let me swallow you up" as other waters do. And the papyrus reeds seemed to sing silently as they swayed in the gentle wind:

Gently, gently, flow gently, River Nile
Move on, travel gently Victoria waters
Go and give life to the people of Miciri....

The birds at Atura flew high and beautifully. When they dived into the waters, they would emerge with fish dangling from their beaks, and they seemed to be singing:

For us, we have no worries
It is you travellers who have worries
We are contented here
There are plenty of fish in the water
And we have no use for money
But be warned, travellers, be warned:
Atura waters are the boundary
Those travelling to Bananaland side
Should know
There is a lot of suffering awaiting them there
It is a harsh world that lies on the side....

The bell of the steamer rang to warn passengers to board the vessel. From Mutunda, we took a bus to Masindi town. Now I could see clearly the meaning of the song of the Atura birds! Since I was born, I have never found a place where guests had to buy meals and pay for a place to sleep in.

I went to an eating-house owned by a woman. I paid one shilling for a pool of water with a small piece of meat swimming in it like a *lacede* in Oitino stream, and a small lump of *matoke,* banana, in a tea-cup saucer. And for a place to sleep in, I paid twenty cents.

Very early the following day, we boarded a bus, now heading for Kampala, that town of magic. We arrived at Hoima at eleven in the morning. We were allowed a short break to drink tea. Hot water in a cup, with only a few drops of milk and some grains of sugar cost twenty cents! And yet back home in Ajulu, under Ladwong Hill market, you could buy a half-gourd of pure milk at only five cents! This was really an upside-down world! A mad world!

At about mid-day, we resumed our journey to Kampala. I sat in the bus until I felt my bottom burning like I was sitting on fire. But I had to persevere the pain because money did not come one's way easily. My knees, toes and hips were now numbed, paralysed with a burning pain and fatigue. My eyes had now also turned red with dust and lack of sleep. I was covered completely with dust and hunger was biting the wall of my stomach.... I bit my teeth hard because I had to bear all these like a man; the path to the homestead of money was not a smooth one. It was narrow, rough and crooked. The path you must travel to get money was indeed a painful one.

The schoolboys and the schoolgirls sang and sang until they got tired of singing and turned to reading. They read and read till they got fed up with that too and tried to sleep. But they could not sleep comfortably because the bus was jumping and swaying on the rough, pot-holed road. Conversation was impossible because of the empty stomachs. The tea we drank at Hoima merely disturbed the hungry rats in the grain stores. We had been served the tea by some young girls. I must admit that the girls from the Bananaland are beautiful, beautiful, although the majority of them are a little bit too small for the type we admiringly called in Acoliland, *Atuko*.

At last Kampala came into sight! It was eight in the evening when we entered the town. Lights were like stars in the clear sky: some were red like large glowing logs; others blue and yet not blue, white and yet not white; others twinkling like fireflies. Kampala at last! The night was not dark and yet there was no moon. It was like daytime!

There were very many people as if there was an *orak* dance somewhere. They all walked with quick, brisk steps, eyes darting like those of thieves.

Look at those ones there! These are the people to be feared at night. They are awake at night and asleep in the day. They are the children of darkness: their hearts are dark, their eyes are dark, and their deeds are dark.

The bus station was filled with people like Gulu town on a market day in the dry season. People were hurriedly bringing down and out their luggage from the bus: they were busy like people carving meat from a dead elephant.

"And you, young man, what are you still doing sitting like that? Get off the bus. We are now in Kampala!"

The voice brought me back from the world of wonder, bewilderment, fear and awe. It was a woman's voice. I took down my luggage quickly and jumped out of the bus. But now I could not remember the name of the man Opira had told me at Atura, and had also forgotten the name of the place he would be found.

"My father's brother is here in Kampala, but I don't know exactly where he lives."

"There are many Acoli people in Nsambya Police Barracks. It is where I am going to myself. If you want to, you can come with me and we shall try to find out from there."

"In which other place may one find many Acoli people?"

"In Kololo, but Kololo is far away, about seven miles, from here. Some Acoli can also be found at Luzira, but again you cannot go there now. It is not safe."

I tried hard to recall the name of my man.

"Yes! It is Obina! The name of my father's brother is Obina!"

"Obina? If it is Obina Selestino, then I know him well. He was once stationed at the Kampala Central Police Station, but he has since been transferred to Luzira."

"And where is Luzira?"

"You cannot go to Luzira now, I have told you. It is not safe at night to go there. Here, look after my luggage."

She went to talk to some men in a language I could not understand. Then she came back to me.

"Come with me, young man. I cannot leave you here in this dangerous place. You and I are both Acolis. Although there is no bed for you in my place, it is better and safer than sleeping here on some shop verandah among thieves and robbers, in the cold, exposed to mosquitoes. Here, help me carry this box. Let us go."

Everybody was leaving the bus station. If I remained here, my life could surely be in some deadly danger. This woman now offering me a place to sleep in was not known to me, neither was I to her. Where she was taking me, I did not know and no one there knew me. But it was better to go with her than be left here in the bus park with these people who were obviously looking dubious. I looked at the woman's box. What a huge box! It should belong to a great chief in Acoliland for storing his chieftaincy attire. I tried to lift the box and put it on my head but it was very heavy indeed. I heard some Acoli young men fresh from the village like me talking to one another:

"Brothers, where shall we sleep today?"

"I am not yet worrying about where we shall sleep today. The hunger in my stomach is almost killing me. Where shall we get something to eat tonight?"

The third one burst out weeping. He was the youngest of the three.

"Brothers, I have here some millet flour which mother gave me to bring with me on the journey. Let us make some

44

porridge. But I am dying of cold. What shall I cover myself with tonight?"

"Okwera, son of my uncle, your millet flour is useless because we have no water for making porridge."

"Even if we had water, where is the firewood for building fire? And where is the box of matches for starting fire, anyway?"

Okwera started crying again.

"Be quiet, Okwera. Do you think you can solve our trouble by crying? This is what you have let yourself into by leaving home, brother."

"If he does not stop crying, he is going to be beaten by us! Does he want to invite on us *kula-abantu,* man-eaters? Okwera, if you don't stop that silly crying...!"

The box felt weightless when I heard what these three were saying. I lifted the box and put it on my head while in my hand I held my luggage. My neck sagged under the weight of the box. But when I heard the droning of mosquitoes, sounds made by some vehicles without lamps, and a terrible noise made by some monster which looked like the millipede and which the woman told me was called *Lerwe.* I gathered strength that I had never had before: the box became as light as feathers, and we walked without resting until we reached Nsambya Police Barracks.

We went to a house but everybody inside seemed to be asleep. They were asleep but I could tell from the way they were breathing that their sleep was not the sleep of contented people. *Ladit* Balibali Obal-lim used to tell us: "When a person does not snore freely when he is sleeping, it means that it is only his body which is at rest, but his heart is awake, groaning under some weighty matters."

The woman knocked on the door. We could hear people stirring, hissing and murmuring inside.

"Who is that coming at this time of the night to disturb us?"

"Nyero's mother, it is me. It is Ijeria."

"Oh, it is you, Ijeria?"

"Yes, it is me. Open the door, please."

45

A light came on and the door opened. We entered the house. It was a small place. Some people did not bother to get up although I knew they had been awakened by our entry. They were hissing, tossing and turning over and over in their beds; they did not want us to disturb them with our talking and laughing. They hated the light that was put on for us to see.

"Ijeria, why have you returned to Kampala so soon?"

"My brother's wife, home is not well. There are many deaths there."

"I am sorry to hear that. We are also not well here; we are starving. There is nothing to eat in the house, Ijeria. And we are all unwell in this house. But who is this young man you have brought with you?"

"I don't even know his name. I just collected him at the bus station to help me carry my box here."

"But you have brought him into the house. Where shall we get food to feed him? Is he an Acoli?"

"Yes, an Acoli from Gulu. He has come to roam about in Kampala. But anyway, without him I don't know how I could have arrived here with my box."

The talk now sounded to me like I was hearing in a dream. That I was collected at the bus station to carry some woman's box, like a porter, a box of some woman whose husband I did not even know! Atuk, *Otuk ruk!* You-disturbed-the-cooking-pot-in-your-mother-in-law's-hut.

"You, boy!"

"Me. Atuk, to be called, 'boy!' "

"Where is your home in Gulu? Who have you come to see in Kampala? Why have come to Kampala?"

"Listen, you woman! I know I am in your house, and I also realize it was very stupid of me to come here, but one thing I beg of you: Do not ask me such a silly question again. Even if some woman collected me from the bus park today to carry her box here, let me tell you that since I was born, I have never been a servant to any woman."

I had to reply in that manner because the woman's tone was

loaded with insults, contempt, and arrogance.

"Well spoken, young man! But I wish you knew where you were and to who you were speaking that way. You spoke as if you were under the protection of some mountain!"

Another woman who had refused to greet us or get up since we came in cut in from her bed:

"Min Nyero, leave the foolish one from the village alone! He is still full of village arrogance and rudeness. He will learn what life is here in Kampala."

I was given a tiny corner to squeeze myself in and sleep. But a battalion of hungry rats in my stomach and the safari dirt and sweat could not allow sleep to come to my eyes. Worse still, the cement floor was cold and damp, tiny insects and fleas from chickens crawled into my ears, for I was sharing the corner with chickens. The smell of chicken droppings invaded my nostrils...

I used my safari bag containing some millet flour and bits and pieces of edibles, to support my head as I lay down eating a piece of cassava which remained from what I had brought with me on the journey. At least the cassava would blunt the harsh teeth of the hunger threatening to tear my stomach to shreds.

At about midnight, a bicycle bell rang outside: it was *wonot*, the man of the house. I heard Nyero's mother and her co-wife arguing.

"*Min* Nyero, go and open the door for your husband."

"I see! So you think he is a husband only to me! What a mockery!"

"If you are expecting me to go and open the door for your man, then he will sleep out today. I am not getting up from the warmth of my bed."

"You don't want to go to the village in Acoli, you are stuck here in Kampala like a leech, like a tick on a dog, why is it? Is it not because of him? We shall see today who is going to open that door for your husband...."

The man's patience ran out and he threatened to break down the door, shaking it violently like a waterbuck caught in the hunting net.

47

"Namna gani inside there? *Min* Nyero! Ladwong! You...!"

He barked like an army sergeant-major commanding soldiers at a parade. But his two wives inside stubbornly refused to open the door for him.

I thought there was a woman with him outside. I could hear her voice and a female voice speaking in English. He then kicked the door open with his heavy police boots. When he entered and saw his wives down, he became fierce like a white forest-ranger barking at the forest-hands.

"Alobo!"

"Yes."

"Ladwong!"

His wife Ladwong remained silent and I was about to answer him because the way he pronounced her name sounded as if he was calling mine; he pronounced it exactly the way Sergeant Otto used to call mine: Sergeant used to pronounce my name in a Swahili way.

"Alobo! Ladwong! Why have you both refused to open the door for me today?"

The whole place was on fire for the two women who had not too long ago treated me like some rain-drenched dung-heap. The women were now silent like broken dance drums.

"What's the matter with you two today!"

Alobo, sounding like a famished orphan said, "Ladwong should get up too... I have been working the whole day..."

"Amuka! Ladwong, get up immediately! You are a mere wife! I bought you with my own money!"

The two women were thrown into complete panic! Their situation reminded me of a story I had heard in my childhood: a thirteen-eyed *obibi* ogre, forced a woman to carry him to her home. When they arrived in the woman's home, the *obibi* said: "Rubu-rubu ye! Mother of Okello, put me down I want to eat all the people in this home." People fled in all directions and to nowhere in particular in total panic.

"Ladwong, don't you want to wheel my bicycle inside? And you Alobo, why don't you want to get up and give me food? I

48

paid two thousand shillings for you to your parents, that's not little money, you know."

The bicycle was brought in but there was no place to put it. The room was congested: children were sleeping in the middle of the room, kitchen utensils were stored in one corner, some firewood and charcoal were put under the bed, chairs were folded and stood against the wall in another corner . . . a *malikan* sheet curtained off the master's bed. The wife who had brought in the bicycle carelessly and rudely pushed it into the corner I was sharing with the chickens. The front wheel of the bicycle rolled over me and landed on the other side before coming to a rest, with its one paddle on my waist. This was very painful because the rubber part of the paddle had long worn away, leaving only the sharp bolt.

The woman visitor who had been talking with the man of the house outside, now came in. As soon as she entered the room, the entire place was flooded with the sweet smell of some Arabian perfume. The sweet smell of the woman brought to me a fresh memory of Cecilia, my beloved.

" I say, the bicycle is hurting me!" I spoke up. The pain on my waist was unbearable.

"What?" the man of the house asked.

"One of the bicycle paddles is resting against my waist and is hurting me."

"Who is that speaking in the chicken corner? Ladwong, go and take away the bicycle from there and put it somewhere else. And who are you, young man?"

"I am Okeca Ladwong, son of Ojok Lapok of Patiko."

"Oh, you are the son of White-teeth-make-us-laugh-in-this-world?"

"I am, *ladit*!"

"Have you just arrived from home? And have you been given water for bathing?"

I told him I had not yet taken a bath because we arrived very late and I did not want to bother his wives for bathing water.

"No, no, no. You must bathe. You must be given water to

wash off safari dust and sweat which must be *mingi sana*. Come out and I will show you where you can wash yourself."

He took me to the bathing room and gave me some sweet-smelling soap to bathe with. When I returned to the room, food was brought. It was meat, well fried, and served with a well-cooked banana lump. But you should have seen the look the woman who served the food gave me! I wished I could eat the meat with *kwon* instead of *matoke!* Matoke may be tasty alright, but it is watery and cannot last long in the stomach like millet *kwon*.

****

Min Nyero and her co-wife beat up the woman brought home last night by their husband. The matter had to be settled quickly before it broke up the family. So, very early in the morning, all the Patiko men in the Nsambya Police Barracks were summoned to come and hear the matter.

"Oryem, go and borrow some chairs from Sergeant Otim's house. Alobo, get the mat from under the bed and spread it out for people to sit on. Nyero, go and call Sergeant Omac and Corporal Lacim. Ask them to come quickly. Alobo! Does your head really work properly these days? A-cock-pierced-the-wid-cat-with-its-talon! Do you understand things alright? And you, Ladwong! Do you think it was your parents who gave me money to marry you with? Listen, the money for marrying you came from our home. Sweep and tidy up the room, and arrange the seats! I don't want laziness and clumsiness in this house. Did your mother not bring you up properly?"

Ladwong wanted to answer back, but she had no strength to do so. She was weak in body and spirit. True, the insults of her husband were painful but then she looked like one remembering how the man had been teased, despised, mocked and abused for taking only eight hundred shillings as brideprice for her. Her father must have told the son-in-law-to-be to stop

50

insulting them, her parents, with such a little sum of money!

Yes, she seemed to say in her heart, marriage in Acoli these days was almost like slave trade. Husbands were like the Arabs who used to buy slaves before Samuel Barker and his wife "Anyadwe" (The white daughter of the moon), stopped the inhuman trade. They could insult their wives without expecting to be answered back. So Ladwong murmured something to herself and remained silent.

Nyero returned to report that Sergeant Omac was coming, but that Corporal Lacim had said he was unable to come because he had a visitor. Nyero described the visitor as an elderly man dressed in animal skin.

Soon, Sergeant Omac came, unlike the elders in Ladwong village who, when called for meals or for some important matter, took their time. When he arrived, he joked briefly with the two wives of Corporal Okello. He could do this because he also came from Patiko and was, therefore, a husband too to the two women.

I allowed some respectable time to pass after Sergeant Omac had sat down before greeting him.

"Oh, good morning, young man. Corporal, so you have a visitor from home?"

"Yes, we have a visitor. My sister, Ijeria, went home and returned yesterday with our father's son. He is the son of the late, It-is-white-teeth-that-make-us-laugh-in-this-world, Ojok Lapok, the brother of Balibali Odora, Your-tobacco-bag-is-empty!"

"Then he is the son of my friend! Son of the bull, have you come to look for employment here? Good. We are all here. Over there is the house of your other mother. You are welcome there any time of the day to suckle, though your mother's breasts may be dry some time. She may not know you, yet because I married her when I was already doing the white man's job. Who showed you the way to Corporal Okello's house? Or was it the Patiko ancestors who guided you to it? This is very good *sana!*"

51

In my heart I was saying: "It was a porter service for some woman that made me discover relations in Kampala." And Sergeant Omac was right. It was the Patiko ancestors who might have guided me here. The woman who made me carry her heavy box was a sister to me. She was Corporal Okello's sister, and the Corporal was a brother of mine: his paternal grandfather and my paternal grandfather were children of one man.

"Sergeant Omac, we cannot wait for Corporal Lacim. Corporal Owiny cannot be with us because he has been transferred to Masaka. I think I should now tell you why I asked you to gather here in my house this morning. Brothers from Patiko, tomorrow I don't want to be blamed for sending away any of my wives without first calling you to try and solve the problem between us. My brothers, I must tell you that I am tired of the big-headedness, rudeness, jealousy and stupidity of my two wives. Look at them! Ladwong and Alobo, together with that sister of mine, Ijeria Acen, are really stupid, very stupid indeed...!"

"Sergeant Omac, in this matter, I fully support my brother's two wives...!"

"Don't interrupt me, Ijeria!"

"Why should I not interrupt you? You were wrong, my brother, to bring a *malaya* to your house last night! How could you have brought a *malaya* in the house when your wives, your own sister, children and a visitor were sleeping in this small room here? For me I don't hide my feeling about anything; I am known for my frankness. That woman you brought here last night was a mere prostitute...."

Her brother now answered her without hiding anything about her either.

"Ijeria! If I call you by your baptism name, Ijeria, you may feel very special! Acen! Do you really think before you say anything? Tell me: Who is your man here in Kampala? Tell me his name and where he lives so that I may go and demand a fornication fine from him! Who is your husband in Kampala?

Do you think I am happy about your carryings-on with men in Kampala? I am ashamed of you! You have shamed me, your brother, you have shamed our father; you have shamed our mother; you have shamed our clan; you have shamed the entire Acoli tribe. How many marriages have you wrecked? Do you want to wreck my family too by supporting my wives who are big-headed? You have no right to speak in my house. Women have no voice in the family or in clan matters, because they are brought home by money or are married outside the clan. Those who have run away from their husbands included! You have no right to be a judge in my family affairs. If you are stupid, I will order you to leave my house today, now...!"

"No, Corporal, don't go on like that. Let us try to solve this problem without quarrelling."

"No, I am not at all happy with this stupid sister of mine. She is very foolish. Listen Acen, we are not in the Congo and I am not a Congolese. It is in the Congo where women pay dowry for men. I am an Acoli, an Acoli from Patiko. In our part of Acoliland, it is men who pay dowry for women. Have you heard that, Acen? These wives have been paid for in full by me I am free to bring more wives, even ten more as long as I can afford to pay for them. Listen: you are Acen, I am Okello.

"That means you came out into this world before I did. You heard bird's songs before I did. Therefore, unless you are as stupid as sheep, you should be more knowledgeable than me. Now let me ask you: in which part of Acoliland do women prevent their husbands from marrying more wives?"

Ijeria burst into a violent sob. I heard her blowing her nose, and I saw tears falling from her eyes. Last night, this same woman was saying arrogantly that she collected me from the bus station! Go on, Corporal Okello, go on! Hit her hard! Go on, bull dog! Bite her hard! Do not stop hitting at her! Go on and on like the Okebu people grazing their goats...!

"Brother, Corporal Okello, we have heard your sister's side of the story, and we have also heard your side of it. I think I am now in a position to say something about it. *Lakini....*"

A letter was brought to Corporal Okello. It was from Corporal Lacim. Okello was given time to read it in case it might contain something urgent. He read it quietly. We were not told what the letter was about. But I was lucky to learn what was in it. The letter had been thrown away and I found it when I was looking for some piece of paper for wrapping my *abugwe* tobacco.

It was written in Swahili. So I took it to a boy in Nsambya Police Barracks to read and translate to me. The letter had said:

Kwa Kopolo Okello,

Brother excuse me, I can't come. I have an old man here who is very sad indeed. He arrived last night from home. He came to look for his son who has been in Kampala for many years now.

His son left home with a heavy heart, swearing to die away from home because his father could not marry him a wife. The young man is somewhere here in Kampala, but nobody knows exactly where. We are getting off to look for him all over Kampala, starting with Kololo. The son's name is Obina.

Excuse me for failing to come and hear your family case.

Your brother

Orac Lacim Cpl.,

Bull's-testicle-choked-a-dog.

After Okello read the letter, he had put it away and asked Sergeant Omac to go ahead and say what he had wanted to say before the arrival of the letter interrupted him.

"As I was going to say, my Patiko brothers...."

A bugle blared out an alarm, whistles blew, sending all policemen in the barracks in frantic movement all over the place. Sergeant Omac took off without even rubbing the dust off the bottom of his shorts; Corporal Okello dashed into the bedroom and was soon heard rummaging through things in a box for his police outfit like a rat trapped in a pot. All over the barracks, policemen could be seen running *ribiribi* as if they were chasing edible rats...!

But that is the nature of the work of an *askari*. At times you are forced to sleep outside in the cold, at other times you have to work in rain. You may be called upon to go and work at very odd times like when you are in bed with your wife or girlfriend; you can be sent to go and work in dangerous and hostile places; you are ordered to do certain things that you would not like to if you had the choice... And you must obey people higher than you in rank without questions and complaints as if you were not a grown-up man!

So, the quarrel between Okello and his wives and sister, Ijeria, was never settled.

CHAPTER FIVE

Nyero and I went for a walk in the city. Buildings covered hills and valleys like cassava mesh drying on rock. Some houses were so huge that you could not imagine they were built by man, and it was only when you saw the builders actually laying bricks and nailing the roofs on new ones that you realised that humans could erect such gigantic buildings under which they crawled like termites. There was no dust because streets were smeared with black, shiny cement. The streets were very broad and were split into two: on this side vehicles flowed in one direction, while on the other side vehicles flowed in the opposite direction. Vehicles in Kampala city flowed endlessly like the Nile waters. All types of wheeled machines were there: smooth and sparkling cars carrying unsmiling fat men and grim-faced women; rude jeeps with men fondling their guns, faces partly covered by their broad-rimmed hats; bony tractors rumbling along painfully, tossing drivers up and down; fire vehicles cruising by with bells ringing, coils and coils of rubber pythons strangling their sides. Motor-cycles were as numerous as bicycles in Gulu town on a Saturday morning in the *oro,* dry season. But in Kampala, unlike in Gulu, it was not only Singhs and police officers who rode motor-cycles. Ganda men in *kanzu* robes and their flabby women wearing *busuti* dresses in the back seats; thin Indian mechanics, their eyes almost shut, rode with teeth hanging out of their mouths. At the points where many streets crossed one another, there were lights that kept turning red, yellow and green. When the light turned red, vehicles stopped and piled up one after another, the engines grumbled and complained, and the drivers burst foward with fury just as the light turned green.

You could not cross the street easily. You would hear shouting and cries on this side: a man had been crashed to death by a lorry. You would hear shouting and crying ahead, two buses had had a head-on collision, no serious injuries, but a wheel of one of them broke off and knocked a cyclist unconscious. There were noises and cries behind: a motor-cycle had rammed into a stationary tractor, they had rushed the rider to Mulago Hospital; but the cries and ululations being raised in the east signalled the chasing of a thief. You could not cross streets anyhow. Crossing a street like that was committing suicide, just like a moth that dives straight into the fire. You had to remember that human blood had been spilt on all the streets you crossed.

Before setting off from Nsambya Police Barracks, Nyero had told me to be very careful when crossing streets. But how could one take care? In battles, you could protect yourself against your enemies, using a shield and a spear. How could one protect oneself against these numerous wheeled killers? If you did not want to die, you must not cross any street.

Nyero was a Kampala child as he was raised there. Perhaps he even knew some of the motorists and cyclists. Perhaps some of them knew his father, Corporal Okello, perhaps a few of them knew his mother. He slipped across the street, and it was as if vehicles slowed down for him to pass because he was on the other side in no time. I saw him raising a hand in greeting to one of the drivers. He stood there under a lamp post, waiting for me to cross the street and join him. A fire began to burn inside me. A double-decker bus rumbled past, shaking the ground where I stood like an earthquake, and for a moment I could not see the boy. I must not lose sight of Nyero for how could I find my way back to Nsambya Police Barracks through the stupid milling crowds? And I must stop looking frightened, because Nyero would narrate it to the women at home, and where would I go to escape the cruel laughter of those bitches? Each time I made to cross the street vehicles would come towards me with an intention to kill! I felt confused and helpless like a woman

57

whose hut was engulfed in flames. I summoned all my courage and waited until the flow of the vehicles became a trickle before racing across the street in the kind of run you might see when a hunter is chasing a wounded edible rat. An old bus came at me as if I had killed its driver's brother! I braked in the middle of the street and jumped back like a waterbuck breaking through the net. I crashed into a giant of a Singh who was standing on the pavement; the white man fell on his back, and the buttons of his trousers broke. His head gear flew some distance away. My loin-cloth came apart and the thirty shillings in coins I had tied there scattered and I immediately bent down to gather them....

Two policemen swooped down on me like waiting vultures who have seen an animal dropping down dead. One held my left hand, greatly interfering with my efforts to wear my loin-cloth. They said some foolish things in some lazy language. Nyero appeared to be translating to me what they were saying but I could not hear a word. A large crowd quickly gathered and they were shouting their heads off. What makes men in a crowd so stupid, so childish? There were men dressed in respectable suits, carrying small leather boxes in their hands. They stood there looking at me as if they had nothing better to do than stand there making so much noise in broad daylight! There was an old man; he must have been a grandfather (if his thing was alive), straining his skinny neck to get a glimpse of a young man from the village. When our eyes met, he emitted a shrill cry! A white woman stood there trembling all over. She was so excited and really enjoying the policemen's interference with my dressing up. I could not hear anything not only because of the noises produced by that silly crowd, but also because a big drum was pounding in my head.

The white man stood there spitting blood. He held his trousers with his left hand, and brushed blood from his bushy face with the back of his right hand. His moustache was full of blood, and he looked like a lion shot dead before it had licked the blood of the kill from around its mouth. His hair was all over the place. He said that we should go to the police station.

58

Nyero advised me that I should not refuse to go to the Central Police Station. In fact I was quite willing to do so. But that street would have to be crossed! One policeman stood behind me and said, "Right, let's go." I waited for the flood of vehicles to subside a bit and dashed across the street like an impala. The moment I was on the other side of the road, the flood roared like the *acucur,* falls and nearly swept away the policeman like the Red Sea did the children of Miciri in the Bible. They had to jump back quickly for their lives. I could hear them shouting in some language, probably accusing me of theft, robbery, murder, rape and all kinds of crimes in the world. Someone lustily blew a whistle, another blew a bugle; cars and lorries, tractors and buses and motor-bicycles hooted ceaselessly. Workmen downed their tools and builders hurried down the ladders and began shouting and gesticulating. Shopkeepers closed their shops and joined shop-assistants. A coughing duka-wallah, his chest curved like a bow, put on his thick glasses and stared at me as if I was a human elephant. If you have not yet been to a place where people are really silly, go to Kampala.

A much bigger crowd now surrounded me completely, but the men and women and children in the innermost ring kept a safe distance. I knew that if I did not do something, I was going to be attacked sooner or later. I pulled out my knife from the waist-band, raised it and shouted my *mwoc:*

Atuk, otuk ruk!
Upsetter of the cooking pot
Your eye-lids are heavy because
You wish to eat alone!

and shouted too the *mwoc* of Patiko:

We are lions
We are a dish of okra
A little dish of okra
Finishes a big lump of *kwon!*

Looking out for a possible first attacker, I challenged, "I am ready! This is a fitting place and time to die in! It's cowards and old men who die at home! Come, you who will volunteer to die with me!" But whichever direction I turned to, people fell back, causing wave of movement like grass in a strong wind.

I could hear faintly the voice of a boy saying! "Brother, put the knife back in its sheath, I beg you, put it back!" Another voice said: "This stupid eater of *mugaiwa* and dry finger-millet *kwon,* what can you do with that potato-peeling knife? The British defeated the mighty Germans and who are you to challenge their police with a rusty knife!"

The loudest voice boomed inside me, "Atuk, your love Cecilia Laliya will soon hear about this! And what will she think of you being taken like a woman?" I yelled:

"We are lions

We are a dish of okra....!"

Six policemen made their way through the thick crowd like elephants through reeds. Three of them carried small metal shields and large clubs, and three carried rifles. They all wore steel hats. Tension rose, the crowd ceased shouting as if some current had blocked their throats and they all seemed to be struggling for breath. I froze with the knife in my hand, and wondered what all this was for, and where it would end.

Their leader, a fat Sergeant, spoke to me in the Acoli language; his voice was shrill, the words pouring out of his mouth in torrents. He reminded me of *lakwal* birds that we used to trap when we were young.

"Young man," he began, "we have come to save you from this menacing crowd. I command you to put down the knife in your hand and raise both hands above your head. I repeat...."

A powerful blow on my right elbow sent the knife flying into the crowd and it might have landed on someone's toe. Someone struck me on the back of my head, and as I swooned to the ground, I was hit across the face, and a hundred fireflies appeared in front of my eyes in daytime!

"Stupid bastard!" someone said.

They hurled me into a waiting Land Rover and the vehicle sped with us the short distance to the police station, the siren and light put on to clear the road off all the other vehicles. At the police station, they threw me onto the cement floor like a sack of cotton in a ginnery.

"Another thief?"

"Yaa!"

"A thief, caught red-handed in front of Drapers' Store. He attempted to rob Mr. Singh Bai Baxis of Uganda Workshop, of thirty shillings. He resisted arrest, and when arrested, he attempted to escape. He also threatened to kill police with a kife."

The knife, wrapped in a white handkerchief, and some coins in a paper bag were placed on the table.

"Did he cause any injuries?"

"No, saar!"

"Did you find anything else on him?"

"No, saar!"

I began to experience a dull thudding pain under my chin. My mouth and face were swollen up, and my eyes could barely see; but nobody seemed to care about me at all. My mouth was filled with sticky saliva and if someone had asked me to say something, I could not have spoken properly. I spat at the back of the door: saliva mixed with blood. A corporal who was writing down something about my case stormed at me as if I had insulted his mother!

"What's the matter with you, fool? Do you think this is your wife's kitchen? How dare you spit all over the place in this way? What's. . . .?"

He raised his left foot and was about to kick me in the ribs when someone of a higher rank suddenly appeared. . . .

"Stand up! What's your name?"

"My . . .my. . . name is. . . is . . . Atuk!"

"What kind of name is that? Listen, young man, don't think we are here to play games, nor are we here to fight with you..."

He stood there, his left hand in the tunic pocket. In his right hand he held a short cane with which he tapped my left shoulder gently. A shiny broad, black leather belt crossed his bulging stomach. I felt like grabbing his testicles and pulling them hard!

"Why did they beat me if you did not want to fight me?"

"Shut up! How dare you....? roared the corporal. The sergeant raised his cane and the bully shut up his beer-reeking mouth.

"Listen, young man," he began his long speech, his lips flapping up and down as unbelievable things poured out. He went on and on like a mating billy goat.

But something blocked my ears like a cork. My throat burnt with poison. His very sight made me sick, and the lies that came out of his mouth cut through my heart like a razor. I wished I could turn into a cobra! They asked me numerous silly questions like, where did I come from. When I told them the name of my village, they grew furious and told me I was homeless. They then accused me of stealing or attempting to steal, or robbing or attempting to rob, and being a useless vagabond. I told them they were greatest liars I had ever met and real.... Three quick fists landed in my stomach, face and back. I was thrown into a tiny dark cell, and they locked the heavy steel door from outside.

I could see mother sitting in the shed of the granary store, winnowing millet, my little sister sitting by her side. They were laughing and waiting to hear a hopeful piece of news from me.

"My son has gone now six days."

"Do you think he has reached Kampala by now?"

"Of course he has, the bus takes only two days to get there."

"Oh, I am only thinking of the dresses and the beautiful beads he will bring me as presents...."

I thought of Cecilia Laliya, my beloved. Some hot salty liquid burst forth from my eyes and poured into the wounds on my face, cutting me like *palabat,* hunter's knives. My body shook with rage. I filled my lungs with air and screamed in anger and bitterness, "Fuck in! Bloody fuck in!"

A communal wailing engulfed the entire cell block: the inmates were lonely, bitter and in pain. They cried in their mother tongues. They cried as they recalled their homes: the Langi and the Iteso, the Kumam and the Acoli, the Jonam and the Lugbara, the Banyoro and the Baruli, the Jo-padhola and the Bagisu, the Bagwere and the Basoga, the Baganda and the Madi, the Kakwa and the Alur, the Banyankole and the Bakiga.... and other tribes from Kenya: the Kikuyu and the Jaluo, the Nandi and the Maasai and the Akamba, and even Indians and Goans and Europeans.... they were all crying in the tongues of their own people....

There was a violent struggle outside. Another prisoner! he was thrown onto the cement floor like a rag.

"Is that also an Acoli?

"Yaah! It's the newcomers to Kampala who are easier to net!"

"New doves in an area are easily caught in traps!"

"Me, me, I have done nothing wrong. It is this policeman who has something personal against me...."

"Shut up, will you?"

"I have not stolen anything, sir... there is a girl that this policeman wants, but she is my woman, my girl, my...."

"Shut up, you bloody fool! What's the charge?"

"Saah, a thief, he stole three hundred shillings from the house of Mr. Mukasa of Mengo. He was arrested last week but escaped three days later. When we searched the house, yards of cloths that were stolen from the shop of Patel Tesa Bai and Bros Ltd., and other stolen goods were found. Here they are, Afande."

"What is your name?"

"My name is Benayo Obina, sir. Please, be kind to me. Show mercy to me, husband of my mother! Now what shall I do? Please...."

"Where do you live?"

"O, sir, I used to live in Nsambya Police Barracks with Sergeant Omac. You know Sergeant Omac, don't you? Please, sir, help me. Show some kindness to me, sir...."

"Listen!" the rough voice of the bully corporal rang out like a bullet. "Will you just answer the question put to you?"

He told them that he now lived with a friend at Nakawa Housing Estate, and that the house that had been searched was not his... that he had only spent the night there with the girl... Obina raised a sharp cry; someone had slashed his back with a whip. They dragged him along the ground and threw him into the cell next to mine. He was crying loudly like a child or a woman, begging the stones in police uniforms to show him some kindness and human feeling.

This was the young man Opira had told me about at the Atura ferry. The man I was coming to live with. Now the host and the guest were both prisoners. Obina stopped weeping after some time and began sobbing and muttering some inaudible words. I cleared my throat.

"Who's that?" he asked, very startled.

"I am Okeca Ladwong," I said. "And you?"

"I am Obina."

Obina sounded as if he did not want anybody who knew him to know of his predicament.

"How are you, brother?"

"Oh!" he sighed, "I am alright."

I waited for him to ask me how his mother and girlfriend and the other young men at home were but he did not. So I said: "Your mother was well when I left home, and she and your little sisters sent you their greetings."

"When did you come here then?"

"I have been here only four days."

"But Okeca Ladwong, why did you come to Kampala? What misfortune drew you away from home? If only I had known! If only I knew....!"

"If only you had known what, brother?"

"You will see with your own eyes, I tell you. You will see with your own two eyes and then you will know what I am talking about. But if only I had known...!"

"Brother, this is what a man must suffer in order to get a wife. Our fathers suffered the same. Some of our forefathers even got killed raiding cattle for bridewealth, didn't they?"

"What's that which the Acoli women have that women of other tribes do not have? What is this extra sweetness in our women that men have to pay so much for?"

Obina sounded so bitter that I could imagine him sitting in his cell, his fist tightly clenched, staring in the dark straight before him, ready to strike down the father of his girlfriend. He paused and swallowed saliva loudly.

"Do you know what has happened to me ever since I left home?"

"Will you two, shut up, bloody bastards!" a policeman ordered from outside.

I leaned against the door of my cell. The fellow just walked away.

"What's the matter with the Acolis in the police force?" I asked Obina. "Why are they particularly cruel to their own tribesmen?"

"These fools will sell their own mothers in order to get promotion. Don't you know that biggest police chiefs come from other tribes? When these fools get hold of their helpless ones like you and me, it is always a good opportunity for them to show their bloody-minded masters that they are loyal by bashing our heads...."

We talked till very late, although we could not tell the time by the position of the sun. Obina told me many terrible things that he had been forced to do: four thefts, two robberies, one attempted murder.... He had been to jail for a total of twenty-seven months, and that it was only after he had gone into jail that he got proper treatment from the prisoner's doctor to cure syphilis and gonorrhoea he had contracted.

"No", he said dejectedly. "No, I cannot return home. I do not want to go back to Ajulu. I am far too gone, far too gone, man. I am a wretch, a complete wretch of a man. How can I go back and talk to mother? How can I ever look my girlfriend in the face....?"

"How can you talk like that, Obina? Who will bury your mother?"

65

A deep silence enveloped our cells, cut only by Obina's sobs and occasional inaudible utterances. My tiny cell became terribly hot and ten poisoned arrow-heads embedded in my Adam's Apple. The air sat on me like a new grinding stone.

* * * *

Every Sunday, prisoners were served with meat, and although it was always half-cooked, it still counted as meat. Sunday was also a rest day for prisoners because they were not taken out to work. For a few hours, prisoners were allowed to relax together in the sun as they conversed with one another. Therefore, Sunday was a day of some happiness and you could hear prisoners laughing. Every prisoner laughed in his own mother language. As the Acolis laugh differently from the whites, so do the brown-skinned. It is impossible for one to cry and laugh in a foreign language because people are different and when they feel something, they feel it in their own languages.

Prison is not a place for anyone to choose to be. Luzira Prison is not a place any person would like to live in. But the place was filled with people like the Pager River is with water in the *cwir,* rainy season. Young men could leave home to go to Kampala to look for money, but when they got there, they found that there was no money and soon they would have nothing to eat. The little money they might have carried to Kampala was soon spent but their stomachs would cry and complain wanting to be looked after like a child. After going hungry for one, two, three days, the young men would start looking for means and ways of getting something to eat.

In Kampala, if you wanted food you did not steal it as you had nowhere to prepare it. If you wanted to eat, you stole something to buy food with. But it was because of this something you had to steal to buy food with that so many people went to jail. Particularly those new arrivals from the village: a visiting dove is easily caught in a trap.

On Friday afternoon the following week, some of us were loaded on to a windowless lorry like cattle into a truck. We were being taken from Luzira Prison to Kampala where our cases were to be heard. On the way to while away time, we talked to one another:

"Friend, what are you in for?"

"Brother, I am suffering for no reason at all. I went to drink with some Baganda fellows without knowing they were thieves. When the police came to arrest them, they all ran away, leaving me alone at the drinking place. Now the police say I am one of the thieves and that I must tell the police the names of 'my friends' and where they live. But I don't even know the names of the men!"

"I am also being killed for nothing. It is a certain woman who wants me and at the same time wants a certain policeman. One day I was arrested and accused of having stolen the smart clothes I wear."

"If the court is fair, you stand a good chance of winning the case. You can always tell the court that those clothes were given to you by an army brother. And if they demand that your army brother be brought to court as your witness, you can tell them that he is now dead."

"I can see that you may be set free. But me! Even if I had had the toe of a duck charm to protect me, I could not escape imprisonment, for I was caught in the act of stealing and I have even confessed it to the police. But our brothers in the Prisons Services are very bad indeed. If this one here escorting us to the court was a Muganda and we were Baganda prisoners, he would have allowed us all to escape. But this Acoli warder here! That is why Acoliland will never develop...."

"I see! So you went to steal thinking you had your father's brother in the Prisons Service to let you escape if you were arrested, was it?" interrupted the warder escort.

"No, brother-in-law, don't take it seriously. It is just a conversation to pass time. You just do your work in this world; it was God, who gave you the job."

We were herded out of the lorry into a dark room under the Court House like cattle into the slaughter-house to wait our turns to appear before the "Big Judge". This time each one of us was talking to himself silently.

"Father, what my mouth is going to say will either save me or condemn me. But if I am condemned and I die in prison, it will be my father's brother to blame: he refused to marry me a wife. If I die in prison, it will be the Acoli tribe to blame: they demand too high a bride-price for their daughters. If I die in Luzira Prison, I will die because of Cecilia Laliya, daughter of Gurucenycio Obiya Balmoi Cotta of Paibona...."

"Okeca Ladwong!"

I was up on my feet immediately like a dog that had farted near its master, and an *askari* with a gun escorted me to a wooden box that was raised like the one for the preacher in the Gulu church. I stood facing the judge. A real bull son of *Ulaya*, England, his eyes were frightening like those of the black mamba. The eye-brows were bushy with grey hair and some hair stuck out of his nostrils and ears. When he briefly removed the small sheep-skin hat off his head, the hair on the head was grey, almost white. He wore a red robe: blood! He wore a black belt on his waist: grave soil! A condemner of people! A real killer!

There were very many people in the courtroom. They sat closely together, looking like wingless white ants prepared for the *ajabu* dish. The silence was so intense that if a needle had dropped down, everybody could have heard it. I could only hear my heart drumming in my chest, and my knees were paralysed with fear. It was so hot that sweat threaded beads on my face, but I still felt as if a spear shaft which had spent the night out in the cold had been placed right through my heart. My heart ached and my breathing changed. I was feeling very cold inside, and yet I was sweating profusely outside. My throat started itching as if in anger.

This was the undoing by poverty, for it was poverty that had driven me away from home. This was the undoing by Acoli

68

marriage. It was the undoing by the white man: he brought money to us: it was the undoing by money: it was too sweet...

"Okeca Ladwong...."

The judge spoke in English and an interpreter translated to me into the Acoli language. The voice of the judge was like that of an angry killer!

"Okeca Ladwong, what is your religion?"

"I...I...I have... have never been baptised in any church!"

"Listen, young man Stop being afraid because fear may lead you somewhere you should not go to. There, raise your hand and swear you will say the truth."

"The truth, yes... I am going to say the truth... the truth...I am not a liar... in the name of God's truth, I will not deceive you..."

"*Nyamaza!* You cannot swear in court like that! Why have you called God's name if you have never been baptised in any Church? Now swear properly!"

"I swear in the name of Baka, the *Jok* of Patiko Chiefdom, that I shall speak the truth, without hiding anything from you, or tell a lie, but all the truth as I know it."

"On the third day of October month...."

"I do not know dates; I did not go to school."

"Last Saturday at eleven in the morning or thereabouts, you started a disturbance in Kampala city...."

"I did not start any disturbance... I was only running away from the many vehicles...."

A burst of laughter erupted in the courtroom. The *askari* standing guard behind me with a gun, shouted, *"Nyamaza!"*, meaning, "shut up!"

"Listen, young man, do not start making jokes here. If you continue playing jokes, you will be remanded until next month. Do you understand that?"

"I do, *ladit.*"

"Do you know this knife?"

"I know it very well; it is my knife. It was given to me at Atura Port when I was coming here."

69

"Why did you carry it on your person on that material day and time?"

"I merely carried it with me on that day... I wore it as part of my clothing."

"To fight with?"

"No, *ladit,* I carried it on me because it was given me for protection."

"You fought or tried to fight with this knife on Saturday, the third day of this month. You used or tried to use it to fight the police of His Majesty King George the Sixth!"

"I did not fight or even try to fight the *askari* with this knife. I held the knife up only to scare the big crowd that had surrounded me."

"Do you think the crowd could have done you any harm if you were innocent... if you had not done or had tried to do something criminal?"

"But it was the police who were urging them to surround me, thinking I was running away, and yet I was only trying to avoid being knocked down by vehicles. I am not used to so many vehicles because at our home, vehicles are not as many as they are here."

"Where is your home?"

"Our home is under the Ladwong Hill, in Ajulu village, Acwa County, Acoli District, Northern Province. I have not been here long yet."

"When the police ordered you to throw down the knife, did you?"

"I did, *bwana.*"

"There are witnesses here to testify that you were told three times to throw down the knife but you refused to do so and the police had to use force to get it from you."

"There was so much noise that I could not hear well. But as soon as I understood that the police wanted me to drop the knife down, I did so immediately."

A number of people were called to give evidence; some against me and others supported me. The judge, with two others

70

helping him, sat there quietly. You could only hear the pens of the three moaning in labour as they produced words on sheets and sheets of papers. I heard the iron sheets on the roof crackling in the sun's heat. The two assisting the judge were wiping their sweatly faces with handkerchiefs but the cold in my heart was nearly killing me.

The judge stood up, supporting himself on a staff. He talked slowly with power and authority, power and authority to condemn or to pardon.

"Okeca Ladwong, you have been charged with wandering; with stealing or trying to steal; with robbing or trying to rob Mister Singh Bai Baxis of Uganda Works Company, P.O. Box 8064496, Kampala, of thirty shillings in coins, on Saturday at eleven forty-seven in the morning on Kampala Road. You have also been accused of resisting or trying to resist arrest; of escaping or trying to escape, and of fighting or trying to fight police with this knife. We have carefully followed your words and the words of the witnesses. You have not denied running off nor trying to scare people gathered around you using this knife. We have established that the shillings talked of do not belong to Mr. Singh Bai Baxis of Uganda Works Company but to you. Do you have, perhaps, anything to add on this? Does anyone in the court here, have anything more to say before I pass judgement?"

There was a deafening silence and I wished someone could speak on my behalf because fear had locked up my tongue and run away with the key. The judge kept his eyes fixed onto the ceiling of the courtroom. Only a short time passed but it was like an age.

"Okeca Ladwong, I find you not guilty as charged. Therefore, go in peace."

I did not quite understand at first the judge's words. He had to repeat what he had said that I was a free man. I was given back my knife and all my money, and I returned to Nsambya Police Barracks, to the house of Corporal Okello.

I narrated carefully and in detail to Corporal and his wives how I was arrested, how I found life in prison, and how I won the case. But I could see that no one was interested in what I was saying because they were not paying any attention. It was quite clear that they were not happy about my return to the house. I was an additional mouth to feed! I had come back to create food shortage in the house, to cause quarrels and misery.

CHAPTER SIX

My stay in Corporal Okello's house was not a happy one. The wives denied me food as they served when I was away. I could only eat if I stumbled on them eating. If you did not play deaf, you would move out of Corporal Okello's house within a short time because of his wives' complaints about relatives.

"What is this all about; collecting relatives by the houseful? We have nothing to cook in the house to feed all these relatives.... What shall we eat today?"

If you were not thick-skinned, cries of the children for food could drive you out of here. The children cried because they did not have enough to eat. And when a child cried with hunger, the mother would bang their head with the ridge of her clawed finger, chasing the children away saying: "Why don't you go and tell your father to stop taking in relatives to eat up your food."

At meals, if you were the sulking type or the kind that easily gets embarrassed, you would die of hunger in Okello's house. If you broke a good piece of *matoke* or millet *kwon* from the mound placed before the hungry lot, the children could stare at you and start crying, and their mothers would shout at you: "What do you do in this house but sit and eat up food for our children? Do we even know who and where your mother is? Look at him chewing and swallowing food as if he bought it!"

But you had to cork your ears to all these and more if you were to eat at all.

Because there was neither peace nor happiness in Okello's house, I started eating out in cheap eating places in Kampala street corners for I still had some little money on me, or, as we fondly put it: My pocket was still wet. I would then return home only to sleep.

When I was at home in Acoli, I had heard people say that there were very many jobs in Kampala, with very good pay. When I came to Kampala, I found there were many jobs alright but there were very many unemployed workers too. I searched and searched in vain for a job for a long time! Finally, I had only five shillings left in my pocket.

I had no language with which to ask for a job, and all jobs available for the like of us were of very low pay, lower than those of porters in Gulu town. But in Gulu town, prices were not so high, although the price of sugar had now gone up to fifty cents a pound. And in Gulu town, when you went to a hotel, you could still buy a whole meal for fifty cents. The good jobs with big pay in Kampala were for those who were well educated.

At that time, rumours were going round in Kampala that many young men were required to go and work on the sugarcane plantations at Kakira, Jinja. This kind of work was not really for people from Acoliland. Most of the workers there were recruited from the western side of the Pakwach River, for they were tough people. It was manly work, requiring young men who were healthy and tough. Young men who had not yet been weakened by drinks and women.

"Opok, let us go, brother; it is better than staying here in Kampala, doing nothing."

"For me, I will have to go come what may. I see no other way out of my problems. The money I had is all gone, so I must go to Kakira to earn some."

"Latim, how's the pay there?"

"Ocheng, brother, are you still worried about the pay? I thought all that you wanted was some work to do? People do not work because of money. Money is paid so that people may work well. Opok, what about you?"

"There is only one thing taking me there. I am fed up with life in this harsh place, but I have no money to take me home. So I want to find ways and means of getting enough

74

money to pay my fare home, that's all. I want to return home for I do not see the need to continue suffering from hunger in Kampala. Ladwong, Atuk, how about you?"

"I think it would be a good thing for me to go because we cannot just stay on in Kampala without any plans. If we stay on here, we shall all perish. Soon, hunger will turn us into thieves and, as we all know, theft and death are blood brothers. I left home to look for money to marry but it seems it is not possible to find it in Kampala. People seem to get jobs here by luck. I know I am living in the house of a close relation, but I cannot go on doing this indefinitely. So I am to go to Kakira sugarcane plantations."

I told everything to Corporal Okello, and added that my mother was badly off at home, and that I needed a job to earn money so that I could return home and help mother and sister.

"My son and brother, I have heard your *maneno* and I am happy with your decision. You know what you want in this world and understand the way of the world. Are you going tomorrow?"

I told him I did not know exactly when we were travelling to Jinja. But his senior wife Nyero's mother, said:

"There is train to Jinja today. What is he still waiting for here? I have burnt my hands long enough cooking for him."

Corporal did not rebuke his wife for saying such a rude thing to a close relative. I knew then that everyone in the house was now tired of me. Nyero's mother was expressing the feeling of all in the house.

I went to bid Sergeant Omac goodbye. I told him, without hiding anything at all, the ill treatment I had received from Corporal Okello's wives. He replied with the wisdom of age: he told me how the hard Kampala city life could make relatives reject their kins.

"Life in Kampala is very harsh indeed. And the women here also can ruin you if you stay on in Kampala. It would be better if you go and work on the sugarcane plantations. Your father was a very good man.

"I knew him very well. Yam-sap-dropped-in-your-eyes! White-teeth-make-us-laugh-in-this-world! In our youth, your father was our leader and I was his deputy. Death is bad. Anyway, at least he died and left you, his heir, to continue the line. But let me advise you son of Bull: do not let women ruin you at Kakira. Go and concentrate on your job and return to Acoli. You are still young. You are good looking. Women will fight for your favours and love. Ignore them. And never put to heart the the bad treatment Okello's wives gave you. I am happy to hear that you do not burn up money on cigarettes like some rich men do. Do not despair. We have a saying: *'lacan ma kwo pe gero mine'* - a poor man, so long as he lives, does not sleep with his mother. By the way, do you drink *nguli?*"

"No, *ladit.*"

"Very good. If you were drinking that alcohol you would go to Jinja and get ruined by women, for drinks and women are great companions. May your journey to Jinja be trouble-free. The Patiko forefathers lying peacefully face up in their graves will watch over you. Go well, *latin.*"

"Thank you, *ladit*. Stay well."

The train does not wait for passengers and once it starts moving out of the station, it never stops for anyone. Therefore, you have to be sitted well before the bell rings for departure.

There was some pushing, pulling and shoving at the ticket-office but it was not as bad as the struggle at Gulu and Masindi bus stations. This was because the train was divided into two sections: one section for the poor and another for the rich mainly Indians and whites. Also the train was bigger and longer than the bus.

There were so many people travelling to Jinja that they resembled *adwek,* young locusts, in a pit. No, they were not all going to stop at Jinja. Some Europeans were going to Kenya where they said the weather was cool, for Uganda was hot during the dry season. Others were returning to their homeland. Some Indians were going back to India: they had made enough money to last them their lifetime: others were forced by poverty to remain in Uganda, roaming about the countryside, looking for things to buy and sell.

At the railway station, there were numerous people, the majority of them black because Uganda was a black man's land. Where were all these people coming from and where were they going to? What made them leave their places of origin?

All the people had been looking for money and were going somewhere to look for more. Some had got enough and were going to invest it. All the people here were working for money. From the driver of the train down to the porters carrying luggage; the passengers in the rich people's compartment, the thieves travelling on the train without tickets, the head mechanic, the lubricating boys... all of them were here because of money. Road menders, ticket examiners, traffic men waving the green and the white flags at the railway station, and the fat-bellied ogres; everybody was working to earn money.

Those who were returning were happy and their hearts were singing with joy. Schoolboys and schoolgirls were going back singing joyful songs. Schoolboys and schoolgirls were going back home on holiday. Some of them had finished schooling in Kampala and were now returning home to work and earn a lot of money. Others still had one year left, others with two, three or more years. Some had failed in their examinations and had been expelled from their schools, but they too would return to Kampala for there were many schools there. If you were dismissed from one school, you moved to another one, as long as you had money. Boys and girls from Gulu and Kitgum, Lira and Moyo... all flocked to Kampala to read.

When would I too return home? I do not know how the people at home were, and they too did not know how I was. It was three months since I had left home. I could not go back home without money because then I could have no reason for having left in the first place. The tortoise has his shell into which he withdraws, shutting out the hostile world around him. But I had no shell, no shelter. I had to find money before going back.

We crossed the Nile and excitement gripped us because we were now near Kakira sugarcane plantations, our destination. Jinja town spread out before us like foodstuff put out to dry on flat rocks in the sun. We were happy to be on this side of the river because we had left Bugandaland on the other side. Those who had coins and could afford it, dropped them into the water, others threw fruits... all because of joy, joy for having left Bugandaland.

Bugandaland is a land of great happiness, and of extreme sorrow; a land of much wealth, and of dire poverty; a land of laughter, and of tears, a land of good health, and of disease; a land full of pious people, and evil ones too; full of loyalists, and rebels; full of witty ones, and of nitwits; full of very rich, and those who did not have even a cent....

Kampala, a city of cleanliness, and of filth; a city of power, and of powerlessness; a city to be brave in, and to be frightened in; a city to be praised in, and to be insulted in; a city to be thanked in, and in which to show ungratefulness; a city to boast in, and to be humiliated in; a city in which to love an to hate, to care for relatives, and to send them away, to save and to destroy life, to learn and to degenerate, to dare and to submit, to protest and to accept, to beg and to rob, to look after one's family and to neglect it, to be charitable in and to be mean, to gain a lot and to lose everything... Bugandaland and Kampala city; we had now left them on the other side of the great Nile!

Kakira, a small town built on the sugarcane plantations, was not far from Jinja. We reached our destination. On our right, sugarcane, on our left, sugarcane, behind us, sugarcane, in front, sugarcane... sugarcane, sugarcane, sugarcane, everywhere! It spread out everywhere like the waters of Nam Onek-Bonyo, Lake Albert. The whole of Uganda got its sugar from this sea of cane. Sugarcane covered every place like the Victoria waters which flowed up to Miciri. In Miciri, the scramble for the waters was like the scramble for sugar in Gulu where you must have a lion-chest, or in Moyo where you needed to be known, or in Masaka where one needed a friend in the shop that sold sugar, or in Kampala where you needed to be an *askari* or an Indian or a white person in order to get sugar.

It was evening when we arrived. The noises we heard told us that there was a great number of workers, and the different languages, being spoken also told us that different tribes were represented. The majority of the workers came from the Northern Province of Uganda: the Madi and the Lugbara, the Alur and the Kakwa, the Jonam, the Acoli and the other tribes. The noises from a distance, sounded like a crowd of people at Lamogi Cotton Ginnery during the cotton sale hours when the Banyankole and the Banyarwanda looking after Acoli cattle brought sour milk to sell to the cotton sellers, and the Langi young men assisting the Indian cotton buyers urging people to hurry and buy and drink up the milk because time was *mbaya*, and that the Indian *bwanas* should not be kept waiting. Although all the workers here came from different tribes and had different physical characteristics, their problem seemed to be the same: lack of money.

All the people working on the sugarcane plantations had left their homes, their aged parents and sisters, because of money. The food given to them to eat was always poorly cooked, unlike the food they ate at home. They were suffering because they were away from home. In their hometowns, there were few jobs for them to do. Ugandans were now divided into two categories: those who were educated, and the uneducated. The good jobs were only for the educated, and the poorly paid jobs for the uneducated.

When I was still at home at Ladwong village, I used to blame people who had unsuccessfully tried to grow sugarcane as being lazy. I remember mother telling me, when she had just returned from a visit to Gulu, that there was a certain man near the Gulu Protestant Mission who grew a lot of sugarcane, but would never give people his sugarcane for free. At the time I thought the man was very mean. But after I started working at Kakira sugarcane plantations, I stopped blaming the man.

Unless you were strong and perservering, you could not

work on the plantations. The numerous poisonous snakes, the many kinds of creatures and wild animals that abound in sugarcane fields, the rough and sharp cane-blades and weed... required bravery, strength and endurance.

We would wake up at dawn when the cane-blades were still heavily laden with dew to start work. Once the dew on the sugarcane dried up, the blades would become saws, making deep cuts on our skin that now looked like the ugly tattoes on the Lendu people. When the sun rose and dried up the dew, we would move to fields under young cane whose blades were still tender. We would work there until after midday before breaking off for lunch and a short rest. At two o'clock, we resumed work until five in the evening. We would then be allowed to retire to our quarters, tired and hungry. This was a daily routine from Monday to Friday, every week, every month, every year.

No one worked bare chest here like we used to do at home. Neither could one wear ordinary clothes that could be bought in shops. We wore sisal sacks during work.

There were very many people working here. The majority were young men looking for money to marry with: one thousand shillings!

On Saturdays and Sundays, our free days, there were always *orak* love dances organised in different parts of the workers' quarters. The dances were always attended by very, very many workers, so many that if it had been reported in newspapers, it would have read something like this:

"Indescribable! Deep in the heart of Kakira sugarcane plantations, the *orak* love dance is held every weekend. It is danced without girls, without drums and without half-gourds. The dance is held not for the sake of it, not for the joy it gives the young dancers, but as an expression and an outlet of the workers' strong feelings. Every dancer wears giraffe tail-hair necklaces, or waist-beads, or large bangles, the kind popularly known as 'there-goes-a-prostitute', given to him by their girlfriends.

80

"All the songs are sad songs, about shortage of wealth, songs of worries – worries over lovers left at home in the village and who cannot be trusted because girls are like buffaloes in the hunting ground.

Girls these days may accept you today
Sister of the young man accepts you today and jilts you tomorrow
Girls of these days cannot be trusted
When they get the educated men
They leave their uneducated men
They claim the educated men have plenty of money
Girls of modern time accept and jilt....

Or:

The bridewealth is not there
Where shall I get money?
To bring my love home?
The beautiful one, wait for me
The bridewealth is not there
Bring the bridewealth cattle of my uncle's daughter
So that I can marry my love with
I have no sister, ho
I have no father
Young man, where will you find cattle
To bring your woman home
Lapobo, wait patiently for me, daughter of mother-in-law...!

One Sunday after an *orak* dance in the workers' quarters, we decided to pass through another place in the quarters where a rumba dance was going on. At the dance, I heard someone call my name. When I turned, my eyes met with those of Otto Luru! In great, great excitement and extreme happiness, we shook hands vigorously, calling out each other's *mwoc* in turn, a line each at a time, as we used to do in our boyhood days.

"Atuk, *Otuk ruk!*"

"Dust-in-the-old-field!"

"You-disturbed-*ten*-in-your-mother-in-law's-hut!"

"The-boy's-head-is-soiled-with-dust-in-the-old-field!"

"A-thief-dies-silently-however-hard-he-is-boxed!"

"The-niece-has-rejected-the-uncle!"

"Otuk ruk-in-the-mother-in-law's-hut."

"Here I am, man, friend, Otto Luru. Haba, son of my nephew!"

"Son of Yam-sap-dropped-your-eyes, is this really you?"

"Me, man, it is me, alright!"

"When did you come here, son of the Bull?"

"I have been here for a long time now, man. I am now even a junior *nyapara,* overseer, for Quarter Number Six, friend."

"I am a senior *nyapara,* man. My house is in Quarter Number Ten. I am about to return home, *bwana.* I shall eat Christmas at home this year. Tomorrow, I am off-duty. I shall go to the shops and buy things: Christmas clothes for myself, and some dresses for mother and my little sister."

"Friend, how come you are going back home so soon? You have not yet been here for three years, have you? Or is your contract not for three years like ours?"

"Brother, if you are a fool, you will die here. If you are dim-witted, you will be worked to death on these sugarcane plantations. You must be a fast thinker if you do not want to see *taabu* here. Do you recall the incident at Onen's marriage dance when a bully wanted to snatch Laliya from you? Wisdom is life, brother; wisdom. I am prepared to return home by road or through the bush. Work here is unbearable. This is a slave labour camp. Anyway, I am bent on going home. I will return home now; yes, I will go home without any problem."

"Friend, how did you manage to persuade the Indians to allow you to go home before your contract is over?"

"There are many ways of doing it. If you want to go home, even tomorrow, it can be arranged for you so easily. By the way, do you get any news from home?"

"How can I, brother? You tell me how I can go home too."

"There are so many people coming here daily from home. How can you fail to get news?"

I told Otto that I would buy some things for him to take

home to mother.

"That's a simple thing for me to do. I know that even if you want me to take home money from you, you are not going to give me all the money in the bank for it will be too heavy for me to carry."

We agreed that Otto Luru should come to my house early the following Saturday so that we could go to the shops together to buy some dresses for mother and sister.

I went to withdraw some money from the Indian who kept money for all the workers on the plantations, but he was unwilling to let me have it. He asked me many difficult questions like why did I want to withdraw such a large sum of money — two hundred shillings. Eventually, and very reluctantly, he gave me the money. You should think it was his money, not mine, earned through my sweat!

Otto Luru and I went to a shop owned by a fat Indian, the back of whose head had folds like the bottom of an elephant. With the help of Otto, I bought a khanga dress, the kind popularly known as "My-husband-loves-me", three rows of white bead-necklaces, a toy wrist watch, a plastic hair comb, one Lux soap and one tablet of disinfectant soap, and a small bottle of some perfumed oil.... all for my sister, Ciri Acirokop. I bought the items for my little sister because she was my future wealth. Therefore, money spent on her was invested. I wanted to make her attractive and desirable to young men. Her bridewealth could fetch me a wife in future. Wealth must be looked after: even crops in the field must be weeded if they were to yield much; goats, sheep, chickens and cattle must be husbanded before they could increase in number. If animals are not tended well, they get ruined and perish altogether. That was why I was buying all these good things for Aciro: to make her beautiful and attractive to young men. I bought some medication like *tutu* for her septic wounds, eye-ointment, M & B tablets, quinine and medicine for cough. I bought things for my mother too.

I wrapped up everything in one bundle and gave them to

Otto Luru, The-niece-has-turned-down-the-uncle.

"Otto, here are the things. Go and place them into the hands of no one else except my mother's. Tell mother to give Aciro her things... no, actually you should be the person to do so. Give Acirokop her things, and mother, hers."

"What about the *ladit,* elder? Can't you send the old man even one packet of cigarettes?"

"We say: a person who roasts eggs knows where the embryo is. By the way, who is that very important *ladit* you are talking about?"

"I have only mentioned it, brother. He who asks questions is not in the wrong."

"You have only mentioned it, I agree, and I have also only asked you who is the old man at home who smokes! And since you know very well that he who asks questions is not in the wrong, you must answer my question."

"Brother, I know that he who roasts eggs knows where the embryo is, but you should remember that he who refuses to heed advice given him will one day go to his mother-in-law's house with his heel soiled by excreta. Are you sure you really don't know Obal-lim, the husband of your mother? Can't you buy him some small presents?"

"Obal-lim only inherited my mother. You cannot call him my mother's husband. Obal-lim is a mere caretaker of my mother, not her husband. Anyway, here is some money, one hundred and forty-three shillings. Give that too to my mother."

"Atuk, physically you are grown-up, but in the mind you are still a child. Let me ask you: in Acoliland, have you ever heard of a woman who has been given the responsibility of looking after wealth? Where do you think your mother will keep this money safely for you?"

"Otto, just do as I have told you: take the money and give it to mother. If women in Acoliland have not been looking after wealth before, you should realise that the world is changing, for the white man has now been in the land for a long time. Look here, brother: there is no other person at home other than mother who can look after my things. Tell mother to use twenty shillings to brew beer to sell like her fellow women are doing. Another twenty shillings she may spend in any way she likes, and the balance she should pay some young men to dig for her."

"What about a blanket for her?"

"Tell her to use the one I left at home in my wooden box. Tell her not to fear using it because all my things in the box are hers too."

"What about a skirt for your *lapidi,* the person who baby-nursed you?"

"Which *lapidi* is that?"

"Your mother's younger sister of course, who else? Atuk, it seems you will get a lot of complaints when you go back home because you seem not to know how to share out among relations the meat of your kill. Do you know that your mother's sister loves you very much, man?"

"She who gives me food, is my mother's sister. She who gives me a bed to sleep in, is my mother's sister. She who gives me water to drink and to bathe with, is my mother's sister. Love is not on the lips."

"You are right, Atuk! For once I agree with you. It is like the schoolboys wooing girls: 'I love you very, very much, girl.' Haha! Friend, how is your love life?"

"The educated men are posing a big threat friend, as far as girls are concerned. Young women these days want men who can earn a lot of money quickly, brother. And the like of you and me who never went to school do not stand any chance against the educated men."

"It is because girls are real, yes, because even girls who do not know even the letter 'A' aim for Makerere boys."

"It is because girls who have read or are reading are too few for the educated men that they marry village girls. This is making uneducated young women conceited."

"But I don't think I can worry very much about these threats posed by schoolboys. I believe if I tell my girl that schoolboys are *lu-ca, lu-wa-ka, lu-yet, lu-nywar, lu-pyem, lu-*any horrible

85

thing that comes into my head; that schoolboys can only genuinely love educated girls, that schoolboys deceive village girls and waste their marriage opportunity for they never have intentions to marry them, that schoolboys only want to have a good time with the village girls to brag about when they go back to school, and that these book boys are foolish and proud; that they only talk to village girls to abuse them. That they have no hearts, they are cruel, rude, really stupid! If I tell my beloved these things and give her names of some girls that have been ruined by schoolboys, and add further that these educated men are conceited, and that they despise mothers and fathers of uneducated girls saying that they do not know hygiene, that the men who are educated are hard to please because they are arrogant, argumentative... she should run away from them when she sees them or else she is finished! I believe if I say these things to my girl, I am sure the girl will never abandon me for a schoolboy."

"We shall see, brother; but don't forget too that the world is not standing still; things are not the same as they were in the old days before the white man set foot here. The world is moving ahead, going forward. The progress in the land is now measured by using the white man's money. If you see that much money is being used, it means the land is growing. Look, these days a girl can even fall in love with a man simply because the man dresses well!

"Well, Otto, travel home well. Greet all the people at home; greet especially my mother and my little sister. Greet for me very, very much my beloved, Acil Cecilia Laliya. Write me a letter as soon as you arrive home and tell me everything going on there."

CHAPTER SEVEN

Like in the armed forces, a person had to sign or thumb-print that he would work on the plantations for a specific number of years, and that before that period was over, he could not be allowed to leave the plantations. But the work there was dehumanising. The food given to the workers was maize meal: in the morning, maize meal; lunch, maize meal; supper, maize meal... maize meal, maize meal, maize meal...! We got so tired of it but there was nothing else to eat.

Because of the slavery conditions, the workers were always seized by violent home-sickness. As a result, running away was very common although very difficult indeed. The thought of home was sweet than that of honey and the workers wanted to go home and see with their own eyes. They wanted to go home and hear the voices of their mothers, fathers, brothers, relatives, and of course, their girlfriends' voices which set their hearts on fire!

Onen, whose name means, "You better see it with your own eyes", a son of the Pugwenyi clan of Patiko Chiefdom, was the youngest of the workers on the plantations. He had grown very big and tall, but it was merely the growth of a banana plant in the rainy season. The young man resorted to crying everyday, and yet it was he who had insisted on leaving home, saying he wanted to work and earn money with his own arms to marry with. Now he was crying: "Angee! Had I known!" He had now seen *taabu* of leaving home with his own eyes. The young man had tried several times, unsuccessfully, to run away from the slave labour. There was now only one way left: by the help of the *nyapara* of his gang.

Onen came to my house one night, crying like a child, saying it was only me in the whole world who could help him out of the terrible situation.

"*Ladit,* help me. Help me *ladit.* You may not know me well, but I know you very well indeed. You are my father's friend. Father used to send me to your home to get him some tobacco. Help me, *bwana kubwa.* I have a very sad story indeed."

"In what way may I be of help to you?"

"*Ladit,* help me, I am in sore need of help.... and if you don't help me, I will die here away from home. And if you don't help me who will? If you are not going to help me, then tell me the name of he who will. You see, *ladit,* I have two sisters whose bridewealth I had hoped to marry with. And even when I was coming to this wilderness, I knew I was just coming to work for the sake of it but not really to earn money to marry with. But... but... but! Oh, *ladit,* help me!"

As he talked, his eyes grew misty, and he allowed tears to roll down his cheeks freely. He could, now and again, close his eyes tightly and then open them. It was as if he was squeezing oil out of them. When tears appeared he did not wipe them away with his arm, but stared at me fixedly through the glassy tears; the eyes resembling those of a snake. He looked really pitiable!

"Stop crying, please, and wipe away the tears from your eyes. There, now tell me what really is the matter so that I can see how I may help you."

"You see, ladit, my sad story is like this: the girl who comes after me has eloped with a certain KAR soldier in Kitgum. The sister who follows that one has been made pregnant. The young man responsible is still in school. There is no one at home who can follow up matters of these two sisters of mine. My elder brother who should have done so is in Pece Prison, Gulu, for fighting the village headman. He had been dismissed from the army for bad behaviour. My mother has also run away from home to another man in Soroti, saying my father was mistreating her, and that father is a poor man. Worse still, father has been recruited into the *luroni,* forced labour, together with others to build the Gulu-Pakwach road. Now home is without anybody to look after it. I don't mind much about home, but what is worrying me very much are my two sisters who are being ruined. They are my wealth."

"The month has not yet ended, brother. I have nothing in the house. All the money I had on me, I gave it to Otto Luru to take home. I could have helped you, brother, because you see, you are my clansman, and even if you were not, you and I are both Acoli people."

"No, *ladit,* I do not want money from you. I do not want any very big favour from you. But, please, do help me, *ladit.*"

"But you have not told me how I can be of help to you. I thought you wanted me to help you with some money."

"It is not money I am asking for. I have enough to take me home, or up to Masindi. Please, be kind to me. You are our junior *nyapara.* Please, go to the senior *nyapara* of our gang and make an arrangement for me to go home immediately."

"How can that be done?"

"We can do it the way Otto Luru's was done. A letter can be written as if from home, saying, for example, that my father is very, very ill indeed; that he is at the point of death, and that I am urgently required home to hear his last words, his death wish."

Onen sat there, staring at me, fresh tears in his eyes. The reflection of light made his teary eyes shine like the medals pinned on the chest of Sergeant Adice.

There was only one way of going home before the end of your bondage: escape. But you could not just escape by running away in day-light when everybody was seeing. You could be caught before you even ran across the sugarcane plantations.

"I am sorry, brother, I do not know how to write; I did not go to school."

"I know you just want me to die here. You know very well how to write. You always do it in the book when you are calling out the names of workers. You are just refusing to help me. You don't want me to go and get money on my two sisters. You want me to die *labot,* a bachelor, a nobody."

When I tried to explain to Onen that putting ticks or crosses against the names of workers was not the same as writing a letter, he only cried some more. I told him I did not have an envelope and a sheet of paper.

"An envelope and a sheet of paper are not a problem, I bought them. Here they are. If I knew how to write, I could have written the letter myself. I did not go to school at all. If I knew how to write even a little, I could not have come to bother you, *ladit*. Father refused to send me to school, that is why I am suffering today."

The sugarcane plantations were very large and the workers in them were more than the people of Payira Chiefdom. There were very many workers but to get one who could read and write was as difficult as castrating a dog. Writing and reading were not known to many workers whether manual workers who used hoes or the *nyapara,* overseers, who used pens. The *nyapara* knew only how to put ticks and crosses against the names of workers.

Although reading and writing were strange to many workers, the idea of writing to and reading letters from home was exciting. If a worker wanted a letter written home or a letter from home read to him, he walked the whole length and breadth of the plantations before finding a person to do it for him. And most of the letters from home usually urgently required the workers to whom they were addressed to go home.

For three weeks and three days, we walked all over the plantations, looking for a person who could write a letter for, and to Onen. When we were about to give up, we stumbled on a Luo speaker who had a little schooling. He was sent away from school after attending primary class three for only three weeks. Ogwang Michaki was dismissed from the school because of involving too much with school girls.

Ogwang wrote the letter poorly, the words in it looking as clumsy as their writer. Onen took it to the senior *nyapara* of our gang. After one day had passed, Onen returned to my house, his eyes full of tears of gratitude, happiness and excitement.

90

Onen's heart was as calm as if he had swallowed some fat.

"O, *ladit,* I do not know how to thank you. I don't know what I should give you and again, I don't know in what language to thank you. Now my way home is clear, very clear indeed."

"As for me, I only wish you a safe journey home. People should help one another, particularly those in trouble. I have given you help in this matter because you are a person from home, a fellow Acoli, so I don't need anything from you in return. As we are in a foreign land, we should have one spirit, the spirit of oneness, of helping one another, of Acoliness; we should leave back in Acoliland the useless jealousies and petty squabbles which are stagnating our land."

"Yes, *ladit,* you are a very kind and good *bwana* indeed. You have a very kind heart. Everybody on the plantation says so. If I cannot repay your kindness, may Baka, the *Jok* of Patiko, reward you well, may the Patiko fathers lying in their graves watch over you. May no ill-luck cross your path. If an Evil Eye wants to kill you, may the death bounce back and destroy it instead! Have good health, and may your heart remain ever kind and generous, *ladit.*"

I again withdrew sixty shillings from the Indian custodian of our money and gave it to Onen to take home, to mother, warning him strongly not to give it to anyone else.

A renowned hunter is killed by wild animals. A hard cultivator dies in the field. A thief gets killed while stealing. A good swimmer is swept away by water. A dark-hearted person dies a cruel death. Kindness and generosity kill the generous person.

Kindness and generosity killed Latina long ago. Today the same would kill me. I had set out to prove that I was the most generous and kind-hearted person in the world, that I was the best problem-solver, a cure of all ills of the Acoli sons on the plantations so that my name may blow like a horn throughout Acoliland! What had it earned me instead? Onen had gone home and left me, the duiker, to face death in his place.

The General Clerk who checked the list of all workers on the plantations once in three months sent for me one early morning. The notice said main office, because some workers were missing.

But what had I to do with this? If some workers were missing, must I be the person to be asked? Is it, perhaps, something to do with Onen's going home? But Onen went home in a proper way....

When I entered the office, I found our senior *nyapara* being questioned why a large number of workers had left before the end of their contracts. On the table lay many letters, all lying about illnesses and deaths at home.

There was not doubt at all about it. This was in connection with Onen's going home. But there was nothing in the letter that could be brought against me unless some ill-wisher had dropped a rotten egg in it.

I was asked whether I could speak Swahili well. I told them I knew only enough to ask for water to drink, but not to defend myself in a case. So an interpreter was brought.

"Are you Okeca Ladwong!"

"I am, *bwana kubwa.*"

"Do you know this letter?"

"I do, *ladit.*"

"Who wrote it?"

"I don't know who wrote it, *ladit.*"

"How did you come to know the letter?"

"Onen, to whom it was written, showed it to me. He told me it was from his home, but he never told me the name of the person who wrote it."

"What is contained in the letter?"

"I don't know much about what is contained in the letter but Onen told me it was about some death that had occurred at their home. I did not read the letter myself as I do not know how to read. I never went to school, *ladit.*"

Everybody looked at me hard in the eyes without saying anything. This made me think that perhaps I had said something that was not quite in order, so I started talking again without being asked to.

"It was Onen who brought to me the letter and asked me to read it to him. That was why I sent him with it to our senior *nyapara*. I could not read it to him...."

"Are you saying the truth?"

"Truth!"

"Is there any person at Onen's home by the name Okeca Ladwong, junior *nyapara*, Quarter No. 6, Sugarcane Plantations, Jinja?"

It was Ogwang who had put the hangman's noose round my neck! He was the hangman himself! So that is why it was so important to know how to read and write! If I knew how to read, I could have read what Ogwang had written in that letter.

"Look here, Ladwong, it was you who wrote this letter. You can even see with your own eyes your name at the bottom of the letter."

"I do not know how to write and read, *ladit*. And I don't know what this is all about."

"Listen to what you wrote in the letter:

To my beloved brother, Onen. I greet you very much, my beloved brother. How are you? I am well. Are you well? But I want to tell you that home is not well at all, my brother in whom I am happy, because your father is dead, my beloved brother. You must, therefore, make haste to come home so that when our dead father's belongings are being shared out you will be present. Finish. I am your beloved brother, Okeca Ladwong, Junior Nyapara, Quarter No. 6, Sugarcane Plantations, Jinja, P.O. Box ....

Have you heard those words in the letter?"

"I have heard them, but *bwana kubwa*, I cannot understand them at all because I never wrote them. In the name of God, I didn't. May lighting strike me dead if I am lying! I never went to school."

"Again, listen, this letter was written on the sixteenth of this month. The following day, Onen went home. Does a letter coming from Acoli take only one day to arrive here?"

"I don't seem to follow any more what is being said now, *ladit,* but the truth is that I did not write this letter."

"If you deny having written the letter, we have here a person who can confirm that you are the person who wrote it."

"Fetch the person. I am not afraid of facing him because I know I never wrote the letter."

Ogwang Michaki was called. And that Luo son talked! Ogwang talked! He really tore me to shreds! He sang out everything without hiding anything at all as if it was me who killed his father, that is if his father was dead. As if it was me who ruined his schooling!

If a black man means to betray another black man to a white person to get some favours, he can go to all lengths to do it thoroughly!

Ogwang revealed the role I played in the conspiracy so treacherously you would not imagine we were both Luo speakers. Yet when famine struck their homeland, the Ogwangs used to run to our home, Patiko, and not to the home of the Indian he was now betraying me to. Ogwang's treacherous words could fill a whole book!

"Ogwang, so this is your true self!"

"That's me, yes! This is my true self!"

"Ogwang, I thought we were both Luo speakers, therefore, brothers. Why do you want to see me hanged?!"

"Oloni, do you think I can hide anything? No, brother, I can't. I do not hide things at all. Do you want me to be part of your plan to make all workers run away from the sugarcane plantations? Oo, *Omai!* I cannot hide things at all; our tribes people do not hide things. That's our nature! We are open people!"

"What's left to hide in this matter? You just go on, make sure you really kill me dead. But remember: your skin is black like mine, but the colour of the man to whom you are betraying me is different from yours. Go on, Ogwang, go on, pour out everything, go ahead and finish me off, for I know I am bitter to you like a *yago* fruit."

94

They said I was responsible for the escape of a number of workers and that I wanted to ruin the sugarcane plantations. I was judged and condemned: demoted to work in the place of Onen for six months and one hundred shillings to be deducted from the money I had with the Indian keeping worker's money. This was to teach other people not to follow my bad example. And there was no appeal, "ruled out by Mulago", as it was said.

This Indian fellow must be joking! Me, to work as a common labourer again for six months, using a hoe and wearing sisal sacks; after being a junior *nyapara* for one year and four months, using a pen! And on top of that, one hundred shillings to be removed from the little savings I had! Atuk to experience once again the roughness of the sugarcane blades! Those razor-sharp blades again! Mother at home was nursing a wild and false dream that her son was saving money for marriage and yet here was an Indian slashing off one hundred shillings like that! And he was standing there arrogantly hands in pockets, telling me I was to work as a labourer for six months!

Whoever suggested that rats become chiefs! Nobody forced me to come and work on this sugarcane plantation. I decided on my own free will to do so. If anyone had tried to use force on me to come to work, I would not have done so! I am a man, therefore, nobody, whoever he might be, has the power to force me to work here against my will. Now, since this matter has taken such a turn. I am now going to leave this place with my own permission! No one on this plantation owns me. And as I have been forbidden from making an appeal to anyone, I am now going to appeal to my own feet. The routes to our home town, Gulu, are not few, all well built!

For the first year and eight months at the plantations, I was earning twenty shillings a month. That meant I had earned four hundred shillings. Later when I became a junior *nyapara*, I was paid twenty-five shillings every month. By the time this misfortune befell me, I had already worked as a junior *nyapara* for one year and four months. So, according to those who knew how to add up figures, I had earned another four hundred shillings. That meant I had earned eight hundred shillings from Kakira Sugarcane Plantations. This amount in some places in Acoliland was enough to fetch me a wife. But now this Indian said they were going to slash off one hundred shillings from it! That could leave me with only seven hundred shillings. And I had already withdrawn two hundred shillings to buy things for Otto Luru to take home. Five hundred shillings left. I again took away from that balance sixty shillings which Onen took to mother. Four hundred and forty shillings left. Every week I had been smoking one packet of cigarettes. In a month, therefore, I smoked four packets of the Spear or the Crescent Crane cigarettes. In the three years I had stayed on the plantations, I made thirty shillings drift away with cigarette smoke.

I did occasionally spend some little money on drinks, and I bought for myself some clothes, beddings, soap, a wooden box, a kettle, a water jug, boxes of matches, a banjo, a pencil for putting ticks against the workers' names, a comb.... all these cost a total of one hundred shillings. The balance now with the Indian keeping our money was three hundred and ten shillings.

So, in the three years I had worked here, I managed to save three hundred shillings. If I had to earn enough money one thousand shillings to marry with, I would have to work for another four years. To make the matter worse, I was going to work once again as an ordinary worker, using a hoe and suffer itches and cuts from the sugarcane leaf-blades!

No! I was not prepared to go through the terrible situation once again! "Chua has said, No! " as our people say. My mind was made up. I had to escape from this slave labour camp.

Haste brings forgetfulness. Impatience increases mistakes. Quaking hinders understanding. Anger blinds and makes one act without thinking clearly. Fussing about things turns you into a fool. Talking too much about one thing makes you become a liar, a reporter of falsehood.

This was my secret plan for escape: I could work for one month, and use the month's pay for my transport home; meanwhile, I would withdraw in small amount, the three hundred and ten shillings still held by the Indian who kept our money. I could travel at night by train to Tororo and get a bus from there to Soroti the following day. I could then get another bus from Soroti to Lira. The day after, in the morning, I could board a Lira to Gulu bus. Once I arrived in Gulu town, I would use "ladeny's bus" – my feet – and do the last fifteen miles to our home under the Ladwong Hill. I never wanted to travel to Gulu through Kampala again; I had had enough of that mad town the first time. And it was also because our people say. "The place you bathe in should not be the place you dry in."

I revealed this plan to nobody else: one's secret should be known only to oneself; if it becomes known to a second person, it will soon be known to four people, then sixteen, thirty-two, sixty-four... and it will no longer be a secret.

On the third day of the third month, at about nine in the night, I was nearing Jinja Railway Station. I had put my clothes and bedding in the wooden box and safely locked up the box with a small padlock. I had tied the other belongings in an old sisal sack; while my three hundred and ten shillings, changed into notes, had been put in the left handside back pocket. I had carefully and securely sewn up the mouth of the pocket. My knife was in the right side pocket.

The night was impenetrably dark, so dark that you could not see even your own arms; it was the rainy season. The cold wind blowing and rustling through the rough sugarcane blades, sounded like a herd of buffaloes breaking through a line of hunters. I was carrying the box in my right hand, and the old sack bundle hanging on a bamboo club put on my left shoulder. I half-walked and half-ran all the way to the railway station to be able to catch the Tororo train.

"The train to Tororo has just left. This one is leaving soon for Kampala."

I was too late for the train I had intended to take, but all the same, I must make sure day-break did not find me anywhere near the Kakira Sugarcane Plantations. I might be betrayed by one of those who sought favours by informing on others to the

Indian masters. So I decided to travel to Gulu through Kampala, "If it is bad, let it be bad": Kampala, that mad place again!

I stood on a varandah as I waited to board the train. Now and again whistles blew; blue and red lights came on and went off... every thing was happening in a great hurry. Everybody walked in quick steps and with vigour.

"What's the matter with you friend?"

"Nothing is the matter with me. I am just waiting to travel home."

"Greet people at home."

"I will for you."

"But why are you hiding yourself."

"I am not."

"The train may leave you, friend. Time is up. Here let me help you carry your box."

"Thank you, but I can carry it myself. An elephant cannot fail to carry its own tusks."

"Don't you trust me, friend? Don't you know me? Come on, let me help you."

"Not that I don't trust you, and I know you too well. Sorry, I can carry my box myself. For, after all, it wasn't you who carried it from where I am coming. Why are you so keen on helping me? You are very stupid indeed!"

There were many of his kind around the station; self-helpers. If you allowed any of them to carry your luggage, he would carry it for good, for himself. To them, "Let-me-help-you" meant "Let-me-help-myself."

Dawn broke on us at Mukono, only twelve miles away from Kampala. By eight in the morning, we entered that town of magic and confusion.

There was no need for me to waste time in Kampala for we say: "Catch and push a puppy while its excreta is still steaming." So I hurried to the bus station, weaving my way among numerous motor-cars, motor-cycles, bicycles and people. The people crowded at the ticket office reminded me of red ants on a piece of meat. I placed my box and the other belongings in the sack some distance away from the crowd so that they might not be trampled on and joined the jostling crowd booking tickets.

If you were shy, you would be left in Kampala; if you were gentle, you would never travel home. If you had a weak chest, you would merely stand there and watch others getting tickets. But if you were a bull of a man, you would tear others aside with your lion-chest, shouting your praise-name as you did so, "Atuk, *Otuk ruk*. You-disturbed-the-cooking-pot-in-your-mother-in-law's-hut!" You would push schoolboys out of your way, rudely and roughly: they used to take girls away from us, the uneducated men; schoolgirls did not want us, the village men, so you would also squeeze them hard as you pushed your way through to the front to get your ticket.

Most people were travelling to Hoima. From there, others would continue to Masindi, to Atura, to Lira, to Gulu, to Arua. Others were going on to Aboke, to Kitgum, to Moyo...

You were never settled in the mind until you got a ticket in your hand; the bus might leave you in Kampala, and to who would you boast of having pushed and squeezed schoolboys and schoolgirls at Kampala Bus Station?

At last I managed to buy a ticket for Masindi – eight shillings and eighty-one cents. I went back to my luggage where I had left them. The box had acquired legs! This was surely the work of a thief. Well, let it be stolen. After all, how many people were losing their things daily in Kampala? If I stayed alive, I would replace the stolen clothes and beddings that were in the box; clothes were not as expensive as women were in Acoliland. Still I found myself shuddering, but not from fear; my throat burnt, but not from mumps.

I boarded the bus, holding the old sack containing my other belongings. The bus conductors ordered that all the luggage must be taken out and put onto the rack of the bus. I took out from the sack my banjo and old stockings and put them on my seat to indicate that the seat had already been taken, before going out to put up my bundle. When I came back into the bus, I found a certain man sitting comfortably in my seat. I asked him politely to leave my seat since I had booked it before him. He answered arrogantly in his language.

"Man, stop being stupid! Did you not find my things on the seat? Have I not booked a ticket to travel on this bus?"

"And haven't I booked a ticket to travel on this bus too?" he replied, the corners of his mouth sagging and his face contorting through some set of ugly movements, in arrogance and contempt.

"But I did book this seat before you and I entered the bus before you did except that I had just gone out to put up my luggage....!"

The conductor barked at me to sit down on the bus floor. So he was supporting this man because they spoke the same language! He said it was me to blame for going out, leaving my seat, and letting all the seats be taken up by the other passengers.

In my ears, the whole thing sounded very silly indeed! Why, in the first place, did he, the conductor, a man who knew very well how many seats were there in the bus, allow too many people to buy tickets? Secondly, this man in my seat was travelling only to Hoima, but I was going up to Masindi, which meant I had paid more money than he had and was travelling a longer distance. Lastly, I was the first person to book the seat. Why should I be the one to sit on the bus floor?

I fell firmly on to the man's right arm, the fighting hand, intending to pull him off my seat; I was mistaken, the man was left handed! The fellow struck me on the left cheek and I spat blood, real blood.

"Atuk, *Otuk ruk!*
You disturbed the cooking pot
In your-mother-in-law's hut!
This is a fitting place to die in today!"

I pushed my hand into my pocket to pull out my knife; it was not there. I felt for it all over my body but in vain. People started doing their silly Kampala shouting. Some policemen appeared. I fell quiet immediately and quickly sat down on the bus floor. I did not want to be arrested again, I want to go home.

As I sat there I thought of home. Which place on earth was sweeter than home? When people are returning home, they are filled with great happiness. When those in schools are going home for holidays, they are filled with happiness. When men serving in the KAR are going home on a short leave or on discharge, they are filled with happiness. They all sing sweet songs, songs of joy, joy of going home, sweet home. However comfortably you may feel when living in a foreign land; whatever beautiful and big house you may be occupying in an alien land; no matter how many friends you may have in a land not of your own, home is still sweet, is still best, is still home.

That is why when you are in a vehicle, or on a motor-cycle, or on a bicycle, or even on foot, going home, you do not remember any discomfort or evil-doing at home. You may have many ill-wishers at home, but when you are travelling home, you do not want the motor-car you are travelling in to make stops at all on the way. You want the vehicle to grow wings and fly you home quickly than you can blink your eyes. You feel annoyed when the vehicle, the motor-cycle or the bicycle taking you home breaks down on the way. You get angry when making a journey home on foot and knock it against a stump, making a toe swell up, therefore, causing you pain and slowing you down.

We travelled for about twenty miles from Kampala and the bus made its first stop. A certain woman passenger wanted to get out. I stood up to stretch my legs a bit, and the heat slackened a little because there was some cool breeze blowing. The tiredness due to lack of sleep in the train from Jinja to Kampala had won me down. I took over the woman's seat. When I was properly seated, I felt my pockets to see if all the things in them were safe. What?! I felt my pockets again and again. Nothing seemed to be there! My knife, money, and other items I had put in my back pockets were not there... I pushed my hand into the left back pocket where I had put the money, but my hand went through, touching my naked left buttock, my thigh....! I felt my face to see if I was asleep or not: my eyes were wide open. Was I dreaming? No, I was completely awake! Perhaps I was dreaming that I was awake.... I felt the other pockets thinking perhaps I had forgotten which pocket I had put the money in. But there was nothing in all the shirt pockets and pockets of my pair of shorts.

"I say, stop the bus! Let the bus stop, I say!"

"What's happening there again at the back of the bus?"

"It is the same young man who was disturbing people in Kampala, he is at it again."

"You, man, now you have got a seat, what else is making you disturb people?"

Anger tied up my tongue: anger over the theft of my money, and over the volley of insults being hurled at me by the other passengers. I sat there mutely, tears flowing down my cheeks freely as if from the eyes of a mother shocked over the news of the sudden death of her only son in a faraway land.

"Driver, let us go. Why do you want to waste our time? It was a thief who dropped a bomb at the ticket booking office in Kampala, but the casualties were not yet known. The news has just been received. That's why some people are wailing over the death of their dear ones. Let us go. We are all looking forward to seeing our beloved ones at our respective homes...."

The bus moved on. I heard it roar and saw it continue its unsteady progress along the pot-holed road, taking me farther and farther away from the money I had sweated and suffered so much to earn!

I was forced to leave home because I was poverty-striken. I never wished to ever leave home; everybody knew that. I came away from home to suffer in a hostile land because I was the squirrel in the hole without a secret escape opening. I was the *odir*, insect without a burrow, shrilling in the open ground. I was the tortoise, the snail without a shell.

I am going back home to a nightmare, to die a slow, painful

death of poverty and hardship. I am taking my bones home, as we say. I am resigning myself to the cruel fate I was born to: to see suffering all my life. I have suffered, I am suffering and will continue to suffer because of the high bride price in Acoliland. Let Acoli parents see what they are doing to the youth by selling their daughters at high prices like goods!

What was I going to tell mother now? She is expecting me to return home with money so that I can marry a girl who can help her. But instead I am going back empty-handed. I am taking home more misery to pile on the misery already there. Will mother not break under the weight?

Now I am returning home, but what will I say to my beloved? Cecilia Laliya, leader of girls, will be waiting for me. But what will I tell her when I arrive home? And when she asks me, "Friend, what now?" What will be my reply?

The white of the teeth makes us laugh on earth, for if it were not so, yes, if my teeth were not white, I would not be laughing today. People say that if you have no sisters, you should look for money to marry with in some faraway land, a hostile world, for the road that leads to the white man's money is rough and narrow. This I had done: left home, worked hard and got some money. What cruel fate was this that made the hard-earned money be stolen? I had put the money in my pocket and sewn the mouth of the pocket securely! Why should misfortunes keep following me....?

"Stop crying, young man. Why are you wasting your tears? Bear the loss like a man."

"Why should he not cry when the amount must have been very big?"

"It was he who was pushing and squeezing people at the booking office, was he not? And it was there that he met his match! And anyway, why should such a man leave home? What is he looking for in a faraway land?"

I heard all these and more. But why blame me for leaving home? They should blame the ones who become rich by selling their daughters at high prices. Marrying in Acoliland has now become a big money making business. To imagine that the government was against the sale of human beings!

We reached Hoima after the sun had set, but because most of the travellers were from the north, the bus manager at Hoima allowed the bus to continue to Masindi. Many passengers were happy because after spending the night in Masindi, they would board an early bus to Atura the following day, and from Atura, they would find a bus to Gulu, or to Lira, their main home towns. But Okeca Ladwong's heart was heavy: he had only three shillings and thirteen cents left. If I had to buy anything to eat, it meant I could not board a bus to take me even to Atura.

I had to go hungry, and had to spend the night at a shop verandah covering myself with the old sack carrying my remaining belongings. I could not sleep because of the cold and mosquitoes at Masindi.

At one o'clock on Thursday, only the Atura waters separated us from home. As we boarded the ferry to take us across, other passengers burst out singing in great joy:

The border is at Atura
This side is the land of sufferings
Here ends the land of hardships
Happy are they who are returning home....

They were happy because they were going back home, but Okeca Komakec was sad, was unfortunate, as his name meant. He had no happy home to return to. No, there was no happiness at his home, and his home-coming could only increase unhappiness.

When a young man returns home from a journey, he first goes to his father's hut. It is the father who should welcome him home before the young man goes to greet his mother in her hut, and then finally he goes to his *otogo*. These people were singing with joy because they had fathers to welcome them home, but Okeca's home was dead. He had no father to go home to.

We crossed the Atura waters. The Gulu bus had not yet arrived. But I had no money left on me. I could have sold some of my belongings to raise the fare, but who would buy them

104

anyway? I was too proud to beg for money so I approached some travellers who looked friendly and asked them to lend me money which I would repay later.

"Friend, can you help me, please?"

"In what way?"

"I don't have enough money for the fare home."

"And who are you? What is your clan? And where is your home?"

"I am Okeca Ladwong, our home is under Ladwong Hill–Patiko is my clan."

"Oh! There are very many Patiko people among these travellers. Continue searching for them. But you should do so quickly; the bus from Gulu is about to arrive."

"Ogwok!"

"Oh, it is you, Atuk, *Otuk ruk!* How are you, brother?"

"I am not well, my brother. I would like you to help me with transport money to Gulu. I shall refund it as soon as we arrive home."

"Brother and friend, I could have helped you easily if I were in the position to do so. But I have money only enough to take me to Gulu and from Gulu to Ajulu. Why don't you try Sergeant Odora, standing over there? He is also from Patiko clan. He must help you."

"*Ladit,* Sergeant, can you help me please? I am badly off..." Before I had finished speaking, the Gulu bus arrived, and there was such a rush for it that I was left standing there, looking foolish and confused.

Yes, Okeca Ladwong, Atuk, you have had it! A song we used to sing while playing in our childhood days came to my mind:

What are you eating?

I am eating *odeyo,*

Give me some of it, please.

Go to the moon to give it to you

I went to the moon

And the moon poured hot peas on my head!

From Atura to Gulu was only forty-eight miles; I could walk

the distance for I was not yet old, although I was feeling tired and worn out from hunger. However, I had nothing heavy left to carry.

I spent the night at Minakulu PWD work camp because it was already dark, and also because my knees were aching and very weak due to hunger. I must confess a wrong I did on the way: I stole some cassava tubers from someone's garden and ate them raw to gain some strength to walk the remaining distance. The following morning, I set off again and arrived in Gulu, the headquarters of the Acoli, before sunset. I had now only fifteen miles to do on foot to our village, under the Ladwong Hill, Ajulu. That distance was nothing...

NOTES AND GLOSSARY

1. *Kwon*   is made by putting millet flour into boiling water and kneading it well into a thick clump. It is eaten with a sauce.

2. *Mwoc*   are short poems that an individual shouts at certain critical moments. During a quarrel, when a person is highly provoked, he shouts his *mwoc* and the fight begins at once, and during the fight he shouts his *mwoc* on hitting or throwing down his opponent. In a hunt, the *mwoc* is shouted by the person who spears an animal. When playing the hunting game called *lawala, mwoc* is shouted when the moving target has been speared. And at the dance an individual shouts his *mwoc* when he has reached the peak of his enjoyment and pleasure.

There are two kinds of *mwoc*, one which belongs to a particular individual alone, and the other which belongs to the chiefdom. Every Acoli male of tradition has his own *mwoc,* and some women do also have theirs. *Mwoc* usually arises from some funny incident.

Friends refer to each other by their *mwoc,* usually only a word, or a line. One form of greeting among friends is the exchange of *mwoc:* one shouting the *mwoc* of the other, one line at a time.

The chiefdom *mwoc* is shared by all

members of the chiefdom; and is also shouted by wives of that group, except when the situation is such that her loyalty to her people is at stake.

These poems often embody names of chiefs of old, names of mountains, rivers sites once occupied by the chiefdom, fierce beasts or harmful plants, etc, which are supposed to exhibit or represent the characteristics or quality of the people of the chiefdom; or they may contain slogans, telling what the chiefdom has been: its strength, its glory, etc.

3. *Nyong* comes from the verb "to soften" or "to treat the skin of an animal", "to cure a hide". If a man does this for you, you pay him for it, but if he does it for a chief, the chief does not pay him. Now, if you hit a person, for instance, and he cannot hit you back, then you might say, you have hit him *nyong*.

4. *Otuk ruk* is the sound of the cooking pot as it falls into the cooking place when it is knocked down. Atuk, *Otuk ruk* can, therefore, be translated as: I am the one who knocks down the pot, listen to the sound of the pot as it falls.